Complete. THE CHAMPION SERIES, NO. 7. Price 3d

THE ROMAN STANDARD BEARER

LONDON: G. FOX 4, SHOE LANE, FLEET STREET, E.C.

mplete.   THE CHAMPION SERIES, NO. 6.   Price 3d

THE YOUNG ROYALIST.

LONDON: C. FOX 4, SHOE LANE, FLEET STREET, E.C.

Complete.   THE CHAMPION SERIES, NO. 5.   Price 3d.

LIONEL OF THE SEA.

LONDON: C. FOX 4, SHOE LANE, FLEET STREET, E.C.

THE
ROMAN
STANDARD
BEARER;

A TALE OF BRITAIN'S FIRST INVASION.

BY A POPULAR AUTHOR.

LONDON:

CHAS. FOX, 4, SHOE LANE, FLEET STREET, E.C.

CONTENTS.

CHAPTER	PAGE
I.—The Haunt of the Gladiators	2
II.—Which shows how Claudius won the Standard	4
III.—At the Throne of the Emperor—The Briton's Doom	6
IV.—Roofing Diana's Temple	8
IV.—(Continued)	10
V.—The landing of Cæsar on Britain's Southern Coast	11
VI.—In which Claudius Fulvius hatches a plan of escape	16
VII.—The Arch-Druid and the British King	17
VIII.—Cassibelan and Stella in the Den of Maniacs	18
IX.—Which treats of the Adventures of Claudius Fulvius	20
X.—An Interview with Cæsar	20
XI.—An Interrupted Sacrifice	22
XII.—Massacre of the Tenth Legion—The Emperor to the Rescue	25
XIII.—An Interview with Cæsar—An Important Mission	28
XIV.—Eumolpus a Prisoner	32
XV.—The Palace of a British King in the day of the Cæsars	33
XVI.—An Encounter with Cassibelan and Stella	36

CHAPTER	PAGE
XVII.—In which each Warrior narrates his Adventures	39
XVIII.—Caught slumbering—Running the Gauntlet	40
XIX.—The Hut in the Wood—A Terrible Doom	41
XX.—Inside the Temple—Fight between a Woman and a Bear	42
XXI.—Thrown to the Wolves—Two Blades to a Hundred	44
XXII.—The Presence Chamber—A just Sentence	46
XXIII.—The Druid's Legend—The Palace in Flames	47
XXIV.—Burning London—The Fight in the Streets—Escape	48
XXV.—In which Cæsar's overtures are rejected	50
XXVI.—Claudius Dreams a Dream of strange Import	51
XXVII.—The Camp Fire—Claudius combats with a Wolf	54
XXVIII.—A Terrible Battle—A dear-bought Victory	56
XXIX.—Death of Stella	57
XXX.—Once more within the Roman Colosseum	59

The Roman Standard-Bearer;

A TALE OF BRITAIN'S FIRST INVASION.

———♦♦♦———

CHAPTER I.

THE HAUNT OF THE GLADIATORS.

"BY POLLUX! good Ammian, this is rare news; what prize thinkest thou the Emperor Cæsar offers to the first gladiator in the lists to-morrow? Nay, thou wil't never guess aright."

"A laurel crown, and a golden sestertium, I suppose, with perhaps the silver badge of a Freedman, if the conqueror be a slave," was the reply. "Well, I am a slave, and the reward would suit me well."

"But I tell thee, obtuse one, that the prize is out of the common, and one that a hero might be proud to win. He who vanquishes nine successive antagonists in the lists to-morrow will be appointed Standard-bearer to the Tenth Legion —that legion which has always formed the body-guard of our great Emperor, whose impenetrable phalanx has never yet been broken, and which has not, throughout ten long wars, lost a single eagle," said the first speaker, with flashing eyes.

"By Mars! a great reward; and one that I myself will e'en try for. Well I recollect that the last who bore that standard was slain more than a month since, at the great battle of Mizetus, in Gaul. 'Tis said that he killed fifty of the foe 'ere he bit the dust; so the position is one of high trust and honour, and I hope one may win it who is well worthy of the post."

The above conversation took place within the shady porch of a well-known *casa* or wine house, that stood in one of the gloomy back streets of Imperial Rome. The speakers were two brawny fellows, whose iron and well-strung muscles, short and herculean necks, and hardy and reckless countenances, bespoke them to be professional gladiators; and while they talked, they took occasional but deep draughts from the earthern wine-cups which stood on a rough table before them.

"Have we any new aspirants for glory in to-morrow's arena?" asked the elder of these athletes, Sporus by name.

"Aye! that we have," answered Ammian. "I was at the spoliarium but half an hour ago, and three new names were added to the list whilst I practised cestus with Burbo, the keeper of the lions. I have seen the men too, and I can promise three, my Sporus, sport on the morrow such as a Roman Amphitheatre has never yet witnessed."

"Ammian, thou excitest my curiosity; who are these new men, and which are the weapons wherewith they fight?" growled the giant Sporus.

"One is a Hun, named Onegisus, seven feet in height; he fights with an oaken club bristling with spikes, each six inches in length, and so heavy is his weapon, that, by Mars! I could scarcely lift it from the earth."

"Ah! he will show us good sport doubtless, but I will back the short Roman sword and shield against his seven feet of flesh and blood and spiked club to boot. Who is thy second hero, Ammian?"

"An Astro-Goth, called Vladimer, who combats with a net and three-pronged trident. He first casts his net over his adversary who is entrapped therein like a fish; and he then despatches him with his trident," was the reply.

"Well, if he nets me, I will give him leave to do what he likes. So much for thy Astro-Goth. Now tell me of the third stranger."

"He is the most remarkable of the three: and comes (so they tell me) from a distant island called Britain. He is clad in strange skins, and his naked chest, arms, and legs, muscular as thine own, Sporus, are covered with birds, beasts, and snakes, painted thereon, with a kind of blue dye, that washes not out. His face is handsome, and a cloud of hair, red-gold in hue, floats around his form, even to the waist. His language is so barbarous that we cannot pronounce even his name, so we call him Glaucus."

"And how may this strange wild man condescend to fight?" sneered Sporus.

"In a chariot, formed of both wood and metal, and embellished with precious stones. 'Tis drawn by two fiery horses, and to the extremity of each axle-tree is fastened a short scythe, which, describing circles with the revolutions made by the wheels, inflicts desperate wounds on whosoever comes within their reach. The British warrior is armed with a longbow and quiver full of arrows, as well as with a formidable spear and a short javelin, and such is his skill, that he can launch his javelin, discharge his arrows, exercise his spear, run along the pole, leap on the ground, and then up into his chariot again, while his horses are at their full speed, and apparently under the entire guidance of his simple word," said Ammian.

"By Pollux! thy account of this barbarian warrior and his chariot interests me, my Ammian. But enough of the outer world; have any Romans entered their names since early morn in the Prœtor's list?"

"Only one, but that one is Claudius Fulvius, the Patrician."

"What? Claudius, son of the Military Tribune, Marcus?" demanded Sporus.

"Of the ex-Tribune, you mean. Forget you that Marcus six months ago fell under the displeasure of the great Emperor, and that he is now an outlaw in the country of the Alani beyond the Porphyric mountains, his great estates confiscated, his enormous wealth seized by others, his son a beggar in all save the rich garments in which he is still arrayed; and yet this very son enters the arena to-morrow to contend for the standard of the Tenth Legion, and I almost wish that he may win it, for, *certes*, he is a noble youth," said Ammian, tossing off a great bumper of wine.

"He win? How can he win, fool? A mere youth, with a form as slender, and an arm as muscleless as a young girl's! I know the boy by sight well, and unless I am very much mistaken he has not yet seen his twenty-first year. Per Baccho, his blood will be the first to lay the dust of the arena. Nay, I will bet a sestertia that I prophecy truly," growled Sporus, with a laugh.

"I will not bet on a subject wherein, were the amount ten times that which you name, I should pray that I might lose it," answered Ammian. "But ah! what is that? A row, by the gods! Behold the crowd; and it surges this way."

It was indeed true. A miscellaneous mob of men, women, and children came quickly along, halloing and jerking at someone or something that seemed to be moving in their midst, and as they drew near unto the porch wherein sat the two gladiators, Ammian sprang to his feet, exclaiming—

"Certes! 'tis the British warrior whom they are surrounding. Now, that is base to mock a stranger because his dress and manners are different from our own. Behold how he moves along, like a lion among jackalls."

Ammian's simile was not an unapt one, for anything more noble or dignified than the aspect of the barbarian could not well be imagined. His splendidly proportionate form was clad in the skin of the brown bear, then an inhabitant of his native island, but the whole of his right arm, breast, and back, as well as his brawny legs, from the middle of the massive thigh to the roughly-sandalled feet were bare, and covered with quaint devices of animals, birds, and reptiles, cleverly painted with blue woad. His head was uncovered, save by the heavy masses of red-gold hair that flowed about his neck and shoulders, in uncombed, unkempt luxuriance, and his haughty face was flushed with anger at the demeanour of the mob, though as yet he had not condescended to notice or resent it.

At last, however, a browny smith, encouraged by the calm manner in which the barbarian had hitherto borne the insults offered him, ambitious to eclipse his confreres in their iniquitous conduct, sprang forward, and seizing a mass of the stranger's hair gave it a violent tug, whereat the rabble laughed heartily.

But he had counted upon the Briton's forbearance too far, for, ere he could escape back amongst his companions, he was seized with a grip as of iron, raised from the ground as though he had been a child, and hurled right across the street over the heads of his companions, where, coming in contact with the sharp angles of the wall, he fell stunned and senseless to the ground.

Having accomplished this wondrous feat of strength, the barbarian calmly folded his arms upon his broad chest, and regarded the multitude who surrounded him with a cold and haughty stare.

Awed by the fate of the sturdy smith, the mob for a moment paused irresolute; nay, they might even have felt inclined to let the stranger go his way in peace had not someone shouted from a safe position in the rear, "Down with the savage; he has dared to lay hands on a Roman."

Instantly the temper of the crowd was kindled into wrath again; stones were picked up, and sticks wielded with dire intent, so Ammian said to Sporus, "Come on, my friend; let us strike a blow for this stranger, or he will assuredly be slain. Remember he is one of us."

"At any other time I would do so, Ammian; but I do not intend to risk my chances in the arena to-morrow by getting into a brawl to-day. After an hour's exercise with the cestus this morning my mentor enjoined perfect rest until the momentous time arrived, and I will obey him," answered Sporus.

"I suppose I must do so likewise," said Ammian, "for I received the same instructions as to perfect rest, and we are trained to such a pitch that the slightest mishap would throw us out of gear; still, I'm very sorry that we can't aid this Briton, by Pollux and Mars I am."

"So am I, but you see we are not our own masters," echoed Sporus.

Meanwhile the rabble had commenced an attack upon the stranger with sticks and stones, and scorning to fly, though he knew full well that even his giant strength would not avail against such fearful odds, the Briton fought his way to the nearest wall, and planting his back against it, with the stout oaken staff that he held in his hand, he laid about him with such zeal and energy that his foes fell before it like poppies beneath the sickle of the reaper. Still, however, heavy stones were flying about his head, several of which hit him; and bruised, bleeding, and half-stunned, he would soon have been overcome and slain had not an ally been close at hand.

He came in the shape of a richly-garbed young Roman, whose helmet and breastplate glittered like burnished gold in the dying sunlight, and who, with one bound and a fierce cry of indignation, placed himself between the brave barbarian and his cruel persecutors.

The crimson plume that adorned his crest, and the short crimson cloak, terminated by a deep fringe of gold, that hung from his left shoulder, waved in the breeze; his arms and legs were bare, on his feet were sandals of brass, and in his strong right hand the short-pointed broad-bladed Roman sword that had cut a path to victory throughout nearly the length and breadth of Europe.

"By every God that holds Rome under his protection what is this I see?" he cried, in tones of fiery indignation, while his cheeks flushed, and his fierce, dark eyes seemed literally to flash fire. "Is it thus, dogs and vultures of the gutter, that ye treat strangers to our city, whom ye ought to receive with every courtesy and kindness? Let one, let all come on, ye shall only touch this barbarian by striking him across my dead body."

"'Tis Claudius, son of the Tribune Marcus," muttered the mob.

"Son of the Traitor Marcus, you mean," sneered one, in a harsh whisper.

But before the words were well out of his mouth he fell to the ground, with the young Patrician's sword buried up to its hilt in his body.

"So perish all who would malign a father in a son's hearing," he said, calmly letting the blood gouts drop from his blade on to the ground as he spoke. "Who next is inclined to rush on death?"

But the rabble, though they numbered a hundred or two, were cowed by the Patrician's daring, and slunk away like a flock of timid sheep at sight of a wolf, until Claudius found himself alone with the barbarian, who grasped his hand, saying, in tolerable Latin—

"Brave Roman, I owe you my life; perhaps more, my honour; for had I died by the hands of the rabble, they might have concealed my body, and when I failed to appear in the arena to-morrow it would have been, perchance, said that I absented myself from cowardice."

"Think not of that, Briton, but yet glad am I that I arrived in time to rescue thee, for I, myself, am matched against you on the morrow, and right sorry should I have been to have lost so brave and doughty an antagonist," said Claudius, sheathing his sword.

"And are we really destined to fight each other?" asked the Briton.

"To the death," was the smiling retort. "I must vanquish nine opponents in succession ere I can win the standard of the Tenth Legion, which I have sworn to do or perish in the attempt. Thou art marked for my last adversary."

"Sorry am I to hear it, for thou wilt be weary after so much fighting, whilst I shall be fresh and untired, and yet I cannot favour thee even in return for the life thou hast preserved, for I have to uphold the honour of my country. I fight for Britain's glory, and not my own," answered the barbarian.

"I ask thee not to favour me; to-morrow we will be as intense foes as though we had heaped wrong after wrong upon each other for centuries, but to-night we will be sworn friends, and—ah! here is a wine-house, wherein that friendship may be cemented;" and seizing the barbarian's arm, Claudius led him towards the *casa*, in whose porch Sporus and Ammian were still seated.

Acknowledging the salute of the two professional gladiators by a careless nod, Claudius conducted his newly-acquired friend through the outer shop, whose shelves were laden with earthen jars of wine and oil, and wherein several knots of men were seated around divers small tables, playing either at dice or the more skilful game of *duodecim-scriptæ*, closely analogous to our modern back-gammon, into an inner room, neatly and comfortably furnished; and here, over a choice flask of sparkling Syracusan wine, the Briton and the Roman, ere twelve hours to be engaged in mortal strife, sat for a while in cheerful and friendly converse.

CHAPTER II.

WHICH SHOWS HOW CLAUDIUS WON THE STANDARD.

Shift we the scene to the interior of the Colosseum, not as now a grand, stupendous ruin; but a vast amphitheatre, glowing with bright colours, filled with a gay, excited, laughing, thoughtless throng, waiting impatiently for the commencement of the hostilities between man and man, woman and woman, and both opposed to beast.

It is but ten in the morning, and the performance does not commence until eleven; yet the theatre is well nigh full, and, at least, eighteen thousand spectators must already be assembled therein. Litters and chariots still continue, however, to arrive, and their occupants to find sitting room, and at length a flourish of silver trumpets rang out cheerily, and the Emperor, Julius Cæsar, surrounded by his great officers of State and a brilliant court, entered the Colosseum, and everyone rose in mute homage.

Directly he had taken his seat, the œdile blew his shrill whistle, and another warlike flourish of trumpets answered it from the opposite end of the arena. Then fifty gladiators entered through the low-arched doorway before mentioned, and marched round in slow procession, in order that the assembled multitude should have ample time t notice and take note of their brawny limbs and muscular forms, their different armour and divers weapons, so that they could the better bet upon their respective favourites in the approaching contest.

There were Retiarii or Netters, swordsmen of the imperial fiscales, spearmen from Pompeii, wrestlers from Herculaneum, and lastly criminals, who were to fight with wild beasts, without a chance of escaping death.

Amongst the most noticable of the combatants were the gigantic Hun Onegisus, armed with his formidable steel-spiked club, and the Astro Goth Vladimir, with his net and trident; but the chief interest of the populace, both partrician and plebeian, was centred in the wild-looking British chief whom they called Glaucus, and in Claudius the Roman, whose proud martial bearing and magnificent costume attracted the eye of all beholders.

Julius Cæsar rose from his throne and greeted the gladiators, as they filed past, with a wave of the hand; then the standard that was to be the great prize of the day was brought forward and planted beside him. It was beautifully decorated, and its eagle was of pure gold.

The mere formalities of the show were now over, and the graver sports of the day were quickly commenced.

Two women were the first combatants, both superbly beautiful, both under twenty years of age, and both of the highest Patrician rank.

They entered the arena naked, save a slight cincture round their waists, and their well-nourished forms—for they were to fight with the cestus—and plumpness were considered an advantage in that species of contest, and excited the admiration of the beholders.

They were named Ildica and Flavia. They fought bravely, and gave each other terrible wounds with the iron-plated boxing-gloves they wore. Ildica received a severe cut on the shoulder, from which blood poured in torrents, but she eventually overcame Flavia, and both were borne in a fainting condition from the arena.

It is not our province to describe one by one the hundred and some odd contests waged that day in the vast arena of the Colosseum; suffice it to say that, amidst the host of the professional Roman gladiators and barbarous warriors from the different conquered provinces that called Rome master, Onegisus, the monstrous Hun, Vladimir, the Astro-Goth, with his net and trident, and Glaucus, the red-haired Briton, became the popular heroes of the day, and next to them, Claudius, son of the Tribune Marcus, who had already defeated five opponents without hurt or injury to himself in the various encounters.

But now the brawny Sporus, clad, save his naked arms and legs, in complete armour, strode into the arena, his visor closed, his drawn sword in hand.

He singled out Claudius in an instant as his antagonist, and, approaching him, struck his shield with the flat of his sword.

The young Patrician at once accepted the challenge.

After a few blows Sporus began to reel, his right leg was red with gore, which even marked his course over the sand of the arena; wilder fell his blows, more vague were his thrusts every instant. At last, with a fierce lunge, he grazed his opponent's cuirass; but in doing so exposed his own breast to the Patrician's quick eye, who, the next instant, had plunged his blade deep therein.

Sporus fell to the earth without a groan. Again the crowd cried "Habet! habet! a Claudius, a Claudius!" But the defeated gladiator heard not the shouts that heralded his defeat, for he was dead.

Claudius wiped his blood-stained blade on his late opponent's scarf, and then threw up both arms as a signal that he was ready for the next comer.

He had not to wait long; a statuesque form, mounted on a noble black charger, galloped into the arena, and, after spurring twice round the enormous ring amid a loud burst of applause from twenty thousand throats, reined sharply up before him, and touched his shield with a gleaming lance-point.

Claudius gazed for a moment with surprise and admiration at this new challenger, whose superb and graceful form was clad in a suit of chain mail, woven intricately with bands of iron, and who wore a plumed helmet, the vizor of which was down, whilst he was armed with a long light spear, whose head was adorned with a tuft of feathers, and a round shield beautifully inlaid with gold and gems, while a short scarlet mantle depended gracefully from the shoulder, giving a picturesque and graceful air to the whole costume.

The right arm of the stranger was covered with defensive armour to the wrist, but the left was bare to the shoulder, as, with the exception of sandals, were both legs, from the ankle to the hip, and by the snowy whiteness and exquisite contour of these limbs, Claudius knew that his antagonist must be a woman.

He turned pale at the discovery, and his lip trembled, for he knew that, both by the laws and the courtesy of the arena, he dare not refuse her challenge.

"Lady, why single me out for an adversary? Know you not that I have sworn to win yonder bright standard by obtaining nine consecutive victories to-day; and that therefore, if we fight, I cannot and dare not spare thee?" he said, in a low, earnest tone.

"I know all this, and I have sworn that thou shall not win the standard, Claudius, son of Marcus. I have also a wrong to avenge, and I will do so on thee this day," was the reply.

"Let me look upon thy face; perchance thy beauty will alone vanquish me," said Claudius, in strangely troubled tones.

"It may not be. Get a horse quickly, and a lance. The crowd is becoming impatient, Cæsar himself tires of waiting, and if he throws down his truncheon, we both perish by the headsman's axe, which would be the mild punishment for our discourtesy."

Claudius knew this to be true, and seeing an attendant of the lists hastening towards the spot, leading a grey charger by one hand, whilst he held a long reedy spear in the other, he sprang forward to meet him, vaulted into the saddle at a bound, accepted the weapon, and spurred to the other end of the arena, where he wheeled round and awaited the blast of the trumpet that should be the signal for the charge.

The instant it sounded they spurred towards each other in full career, and met with a shock in the very centre of the lists.

Claudius had directed his lance point at the thick round shield that covered his fair antagonist's bosom, hoping to unhorse her, and that she would accept that slight reverse as the termination of the fray; but his frail reed-like spear shivered to fragments against the stout iron, whilst the lady scarcely reeled in her saddle, and the point of her weapon, missing his undefended brow by just an inch, struck the helmet from his head with no gentle force, amid the loud applause of the spectators.

The unknown then dropped her lance to the ground, and drawing her sword attacked Claudius with great energy. The young Patrician guarded all her cuts and thrusts with consummate skill for many minutes, without striking a blow in return, whilst the horses reared and plunged and bit fiercely at each other, as if they delighted in the fray as much as their riders.

At length Claudius saw that to save his own life, and rid himself of his adversary, he must wound or disable her in some way. Seizing his opportunity, he struck a vigorous blow at her sword-hilt, hoping to dash the weapon from her grasp; but, owing to a sudden movement of her horse, the sword-blade glanced down upon her beautiful snow-white exquisitely-rounded thigh, cutting the soft flesh open to the bone.

Her sword fell from her relaxed grasp, she uttered a loud cry of pain, and, dropping the reins, crashed down in all her steel panoply upon the sands of the arena.

Claudius was by her side in an instant, unlacing her helm; it at last fell off, revealing a face of exquisite and youthful beauty, and permitting a perfect cloud of golden curls to flow over her armour.

"Heavens! the Lady Eudochia, my promised bride!" exclaimed Claudius, aghast, as he fell on his knees by her side, and strove to restore her to consciousness.

But the attendants of the arena came quickly up, and bore her away to be tended by the surgeons, and the next instant it was notified to the young Patrician that the Emperor desired his presence before his throne.

To hear was to obey, and resuming his glittering and plumed helmet, Claudius restored his sword to its sheath, and, with proud and haughty gait, approached the golden throne of Cæsar, and bent gracefully on one knee before the Emperor.

"Thou hast already been triumphant over six antagonists, and now, instead of being the challenged, have the right in turn to become the challenger. If thou achievest three more victories, the golden standard of the Tenth Legion is yours," said Julius Cæsar, in a kindly tone of voice. "Whom wilt thou select to fight with?"

"My Emperor, I will choose the three most formidable antagonists in the arena; the giant Hun with his spiken club, the Astro-Goth, with his net and trident; and, lastly, the British Chief, who in his swift war-chariot hath already slain a dozen gladiators," answered Claudius, proudly.

"Boy, I like thy spirit; go and fight these men; an inner conviction tells me that thou wilt come off victor," said Cæsar, approvingly, and then Claudius kissed his hand, bowed himself backwards to a distance of about a dozen yards from the throne, and then turning on his heel, he proceeded to challenge the dark-browed Hun to mortal combat.

This giant had already slain four Roman gladiators, and had not once suffered defeat in turn, but Claudius made short work of him, for avoiding his terrible weapon by a series of agile and cat-like springs, he inflicted so many wounds with the point of his sword, that the bulky Hun at last fell to the earth from mere loss of blood, and was dispatched with ease.

The Patrician, his sword still red with the giant Hun's blood, now mounted a strong powerful charger, that was provided him for the purpose, and rode up to where the Astro-Goth, Vladimir, sat on his great white horse, the butt end of his long trident resting on his foot, his net flung carelessly over his left shoulder, looking like a colossal Titan hewn from marble.

Claudius made just as short work with Vladimir as he had done with Sporus, and then prepared to meet the British chief.

The Briton, stern, calm, immovable, expressionless as a North-American Indian of the present day, and equally as wild and majestic in appearance, stood in his war chariot, with his bow, and his quiver full of arrows, his javelin and his spear, ready and eager for the contest.

His red, gold hair hung in a cloud around him, and his cloak of skins dropped as majestically from his brawny shoulder as though it had been the regal purple of an Emperor.

Claudius thought for a moment how he could best oppose this strange adversary, and he at last selected a horse and a lance of tough ash wood, and mounting, rode up and saluted him with—

"Barbarian, our short term of friendship is over, we must now to mortal strife, thou for the honour of thy country, I for the standard that I have sworn to win, or die in the attempt. Art thou ready?"

"Quite noble Roman, and I have been keeping my hand in by slaying eight of thy tried gladiators; so you perceive we have each had equally hard labour, and are, I daresay, about equally fatigued. Still, let us hasten to the contest, for the Emperor and the people wait. But first, thy hand."

The two warriors clasped hands, and then they wheeled round and repaired to their appointed posts at opposite ends of the arena.

The trumpets rang shrilly out, and they approached each other like two thunderbolts, the British chariot-wheels revolving so quickly that the spokes could scarcely be seen, while the flashing scythes glittered like lightning.

CHAPTER III.

AT THE THRONE OF THE EMPEROR.—THE BRITON'S DOOM.

THE Roman's lance was levelled at the Briton's breast, but ere he could approach the chariot, the fatal javelin was hurled, and his charger fell to the ground, pierced through the heart.

Ere he could disengage himself from the fallen animal the chariot rushed by with a clatter and roar, and one of its revolving scythes cut deep into his left leg, whilst the Briton's spear shattered against his corselet of proof.

But he was ready to renew the contest in an instant, and when the chariot wheeled round and drawn by its two snorting fiery horses again rushed towards him, he seized his opportunity and thrust his sword deep into one of the animal's shoulders as it passed him, and thereafter avoiding being cut down by one of the revolving scythes by next to a miracle, with a single bound he was inside the chariot and opposed to the savage Briton in a hand-to-hand fight.

For a good five minutes they struggled on the Roman sword opposed to the British axe, wounds were given and taken freely on either side, and a mixed puddle of Roman and British blood collected at the bottom of the chariot, which the maddened horses continued to propel across and around the vast arena as they listed.

At last the Roman was beaten to his knee, but springing up he grasped the brawny arm that wielded the death-dealing axe, and arrest its descending sweep. Then they grappled and reeled out of the chariot on to the sands of the arena. Both weapons were, by this time, cast aside, and on thews and sinews depended the fate of the day. The struggle was that of two Samsons, but at length the Briton stepped on the blade of his own axe, cut his foot to the bone, and fell to the ground.

The Roman's knee was upon his broad breast in an instant, and in a voice of thunder he called upon him to yield.

"I do yield," answered the barbarian, "let us be friends again, Claudius?"

"Aye, for life, if thou wilt," was the reply, as our hero seized the proffered hand.

Then one loud and prolonged cheer shook the very walls of the great amphitheatre, and Julius Cæsar, rising to his feet, proclaimed that Claudius, son of the Tribune Marcus, was Champion of the Arena and Standard Bearer to the Tenth Legion.

And Claudius was led by the Edile and the Editor of the Sports to the throne of Cæsar, and he knelt on the ivory daïs, and the great conqueror of nations took the golden-eagled standard and placed it in his hand, saying—

"Noble youth, to your care I entrust my most prized of standards, the standard of the legion that has never been defeated, never repulsed, never lost its honour or its eagle. It has been held by many brave men, and its last guardian slew fifty Gauls in its defence on the bloody field of Mizetus, yet I am convinced that you will uphold it with equal credit when the occasion arises."

Claudius bowed, and accepted the standard from the hands of the monarch, saying—"With such examples before me, I will try to be equally worthy, my Emperor."

"Who art thou, youth?" asked Julius Cæsar, with some interest. "Thou hast the air, the manner, the address of a Patrician, and art no common gladiator, I dare swear."

"I'm Claudius Fulvius, son of the Military Tribune Marcus, at present in banishment in the country of the Alani," answered our hero, calmly.

"Then thou art the son of a traitor," said Cæsar, his brow darkening.

"Marcus the Tribune is no traitor," answered Claudius, springing to his feet, unconscious of the presence in which he stood. "I, his son, swear it."

"By the gods! boy, thou art as full of fire as the crater of Vesuvius!" exclaimed Julius Cæsar, half in anger, half in admiration, at the young Patrician's courage; "know you not that the punishment is death for speaking thus in the presence of your Emperor? But on this occasion I forgive thee, for thou seemest jealous of thy father's honour, and on that account art the more likely to guard well thine own, and that of thy Legion. Go, I have said it."

With a deep bow Claudius, banner in hand, withdrew from the Imperial presence, and then Cæsar commanded the Prætors to bring before him the red-haired barbarian, Glaucus.

In obedience to the mandate, the Briton the next minute stood in the Imperial presence erect and undaunted, his hair floating around his neck and shoulders like a glory, his features calm, dignified, and king-like. He refused to bend the knee in homage to the conquerer of half the world.

"Barbarian, dost thou refuse to kneel to an Emperor, whose train crowned kings have been proud to uphold?" asked Cæsar.

"Aye! that do I, most mighty Emperor; let the conquered kneel, be they kings or serfs; but I come from a land on whose shores the invader has never placed his foot, a land wherein all men are free, and where we bow the knee but to the gods we serve," was the reply.

"Barbarian, thou speakest boldly; didst thou journey to Rome in order to brow-beat us on our very throne; few monarchs would have dared thus to have spoken to Cæsar. Why didst thou come here?"

"I came not hither, O conqueror of nations, to contend with the beasts that perish, but with the best swordsmen and warriors that Rome could produce. Of them I, an untutored savage, as, doubtless thou deemest me, have slain eight out of my nine adversaries. Methinks that is enough for one day; yet, if thou wilt promise me to abandon thy insane project to conquer Britain, I will, to show the power that dwells in a Briton's arm, encounter thy Numidian lion, aye, and every wild beast in thy imperial menagerie in succession, if thou choosest," answered the barbarian, with a laugh.

Julius Cæsar started in amazement.

He could scarcely imagine that the barbarian who spoke so calmly could really mean what he said.

Not one man in a thousand who contended with a lion, with the primitive weapons then in use, came off victorious; so he answered, with a smile—

"I promise thee, Briton, that, if thou slayest the Numidian lion, thou shalt thereby win deliverance for thy nation from Roman thraldom. If thou conquerest the lion thou wilt make Cæsar feel such a respect for the people thou representest, that they shall be his brethren instead of his foes. So the Emperor has spoken!"

"And he has spoken as the Emperor of such a nation as Rome should speak—kingly, nobly!" was the reply. "The lion shall die by my hand!"

*   *   *   *   *

Five minutes later, armed with a short Roman sword, and having a cloak of skins wrapped around his upraised left arm, the Briton knelt on one knee in the arena, and awaited the attack of the king of beasts.

An immense cage, or rather grated den, was now drawn by four horses into the very centre of the arena, and the next moment the roar of the great lion struck upon the ears of the multitude, many of whom could see his gaunt form and great maned head, as it snuffed at the air through the strong bars, and strode up and down its narrow confined prison, as though impatient to be free.

Then the horses were led away, and the keeper of the lion cautiously drew up the grating of the cage, and hastily retreated through the grated passage leading from the arena, and left the lion and the Briton alone in the lists.

With one fierce bound the king of beasts leapt

at least half a dozen yards from his den, and then stood glaring defiantly around, and lashing his sides with his long tail.

Then it raised itself half on end, and eagerly snuffed the air, thereafter starting in a mad race round and round the arena, uttering roars of baffled rage and disappointment as it found every avenue of escape barred.

During all this while the Briton continued to turn as if on a pivot, never taking his eye from, or turning his back on the king of beasts for a moment; and well was it that he did so, for suddenly, and without any warning of its intention, the lion ceased its rapid circular gyrations, and, like an arrow shot from a Parthian bow, darted down upon its prey.

The Briton regarded the beast's swift advance with unblanched cheek and undismayed front—and, as with red gleaming eyes and open jaws and bristling mane, it rushed upon him a dozen feet at a bound, he leant well forward still on one knee, and his left skin-protected arm raised to guard his throat, while he grasped the short Roman sword so tightly in his right hand, with its point threatening its fell foe, that every vein and muscle right up to his massive shoulder stood out like whipcord.

Nearer and nearer, with angry roars and a succession of bounds that scattered the yellow sands of the arena, as the prow of a swift ship scatters the ocean spray, came the lion. A breathless silence o'erspread the twenty thousand spectators as with a pall; then suddenly women shrieked, and even stern men gave vent to a stifled gasp of horror, for man and beast had met in the fatal struggle, and for a moment a cloud of dust hid both from view.

When it cleared away a shout so loud, so strong, so fierce in joy and rapture, that it seemed to make the vast amphitheatre shake to its foundations, arose from that vast assemblage—with one accord each human unit sprang to his or her feet and joined in the thrilling cry; for lo! the mighty lion, lately so terrible in its magnificent strength, lay quivering in his death agony on the sand, and the Briton stood towering over him, a calm smile irradiating his countenance as he held aloft a sword crimson from point to hilt, the great blood gouts from which fell adown his naked arm and reddened the sand of the arena.

The death of the lion had been instantaneous, the fierce brute had sprung at the Briton's throat, but had been caught upon his left arm, trebly protected by thick bear skins, and the same instant the broad-bladed sword had been thrust into its heart up to the very hilt.

"A Glaucus! A Glaucus! King of the Arena and of the Lions!" shouted the editor of the sports, carried away by an enthusiasm that he could not repress, and the cry was echoed and re-echoed until it rang through the length and breadth of Imperial Rome.

Again was the Briton led up to the throne of Cæsar, again was he congratulated by that monarch on the prowess he had displayed; but the brow of the Emperor was nevertheless clouded, for he remembered the promise he had made, that if the Briton should slay the lion, he should thereby win for his nation deliverance from Roman attack and Roman thraldom; and he felt wrathful and incensed against himself for having made such a promise; for Cæsar had vowed to conquer Britain and recruit his army with her warlike sons, for he felt that, with Roman discipline and Roman arms, a legion of such men would be invincible, and the prowess, strength, and true heroism shown by Glaucus that day in the arena made him more intent than ever upon accomplishing this pet scheme, and to do it without further delay.

The sports of the arena were now over, and the Emperor and his brilliant train setting the example, the vast multitude slowly quitted the Amphitheatre.

CHAPTER IV.
ROOFING DIANA'S TEMPLE.

CHANGE we the scene to the seagirt Isle of Britain, to the interior of one of its mighty forests, wherein stands the temple of the great Goddess Diana. Twelve long months have flown by since the events recorded in our last chapter, and again it is the glorious summer time.

It is early morn, the sun has just risen, and its glittering rays fall upon the walls and roof of a temple that stands in a beautiful and grassy glade, surrounded by a circle of giant oak trees.

Its walls are of stone, and in many parts thereof are there attempts at rude carving, whilst its roof is composed of slabs of wood, laid on like shingles, and nailed together in some rude but effectual fashion.

The whole scene presents an appearance of singular beauty and solitude; but suddenly it is enlivened by human voices, and a troop of young maidens emerge from amidst the trees, and in procession glide towards the temple with quick and joyous tread.

The foremost of this beautiful troop bears aloft a standard white as snow, and each of the other maidens carries in one hand a kind of basket full of oak slabs, in the other a hammer, and from the girdle of each glitters the hilt of a dagger studded with precious stones.

These girls, a hundred in number, are priestesses of the great goddess Diana, and they are about to perform the great annual ceremony of uncovering and re-roofing her temple in one day.

See at a given point, marked by a solitary sycamore tree, they halt; there is a pause for a few minutes, and then their leader raises her standard thrice, the third time uttering a shrill cry.

The ladders are placed against the walls of the temple, nowhere more than about twelve feet in height, and the priestesses swarm up them on to the roof.

The arch-priestess is the last to ascend, and having gained the summit she slowly and deliberately, with a piece of chalk, divides the nearly flat roof into ninety-eight squares, one for each priestess, which she has to divest of the old tiles and recover with the new before the sun sinks below the horizon.

This measuring and marking out accomplished,

the young girls, not one of whom has attained her twentieth year, set to work with a will, for they know that each one who has not finished her task at the appointed time will be burnt alive as an offering to the inexorable goddess.

Hour after hour rolls on—the sun rises higher and higher in the heavens—and still the work goes on bravely. The heat is intense, but the priestesses never slacken their labours for an instant, and the ring of their hammers is incessant.

For fifteen hours they toiled and toiled, without food or water passing their lips. Sometimes one would fall down in a faint, but her companions would promptly restore her with a prick of a dagger or the blow of a hammer on arm, hip, or thigh, and she would set to work again harder than ever to make up for lost time.

At last evening drew on, and many a face grew anxious as the shadows lengthened on the green sward, for it wanted but an hour to sunset, and the work was not yet nearly finished.

Would it be done in time?

It was an hour of intense excitement.

How quick the hammers rang, while a hundred rounded arms rose and fell in rapid undulation, and chests heaved and bosoms throbbed, and frightened hearts could be seen wildly beating beneath creamy blue-veined skins, while on many a swaying bust and rounded hip the perspiration dwelt like dewdrops.

At last a cry from the arch-priestess, long and shrill as a muezzin's call to prayers in a Moslem city, and the sudden elevation of the white standard proclaimed that the sun had set, and in an instant every hammer ceased to strike, and every beautiful artificer seemed turned into stone.

Then a wail of despair arose to the deep blue heavens, for no less than nine out of those ninety-eight virgins had failed to complete their task by the appointed hour, and they knew that their doom was a terrible death.

The arch-priests detected them in an instant, and ordered that they should be bound.

Vain were their shrieks, their prayers, their entreaties.

Their co-workers sprang upon them, and girt them with cruel thongs that cut deep into their delicate flesh.

They were then forced down the ladders, and while sundry of the virgins descending after them commenced to build their funeral pyres at the lower end of the glade, others remained on the roof to complete that which the unfortunates had been unable to effect.

An hour passed by, and the pale moon, in place of the radiant sun, arose, and shed its calm holy light upon the scene.

The funeral pyres had been erected, nine in a row, consisting each of a stake thrust upright in the ground, to which a victim was to be bound, surrounded by piles of wood and faggots, that only awaited the match to burst instantly into flame.

At length strains of barbaric music were audible in the distance, each moment approaching nearer and nearer. Then suddenly they ceased, or rather changed into a rude chaunt, whose swelling

chests approached the altar.

Nine times did they walk round oak tree, altar, and funeral pyres, in solemn and slow array, still singing their monotonous chaunt, and then their gaunt and aged leader drew a golden sickle from beneath his spotless robes, and cut from the lowest branch of the old oak one of the boughs of white-budded mistletoe.

This he cast upon the blue-flamed altar fire, wherein it crackled and was shrivelled up in an instant. When not a trace of it remained he cried in a solemn and loud voice—

"Bring the victims forth."

In immediate response to the call each surrounding tree seemed to give birth to a beautiful and white-robed priestess, as one by one they appeared from behind their giant trunks and advanced towards the grim circle of bearded Druids.

Amongst them, their arms pinioned behind their backs, walked the nine prisoners, with mournful but resigned aspect, with slow but solemn steps. They gazed upon the stakes and the faggots without a shudder, and yet it was hard to die whilst so young and so beautiful.

They must have felt this, yet they never quailed nor suffered any outer manifestation of fear to escape them, but walked fearlessly up to the Arch-Druid and knelt before him and the blue-flamed altar fire.

He regarded them sternly for an instant, then addressed a few words to each in turn, and taking a brand from the fire, scattered a thousand glittering sparks over their naked bodies. Next he gave each one a cross gash over the left shoulder with the point of his golden sickle, and ordered them forthwith to be bound to the stakes and the flames applied thereto.

They were led away, supported by priestesses, and in less than five minutes they stood chained to the stakes, and the flames leaped up madly around them. Their last hour had come.

Their last hour! aye, almost their last minute! for death by fire is swift and terrible, and the faggots and stacks of wood being dry as tinder, sprang into rampant life with amazing velocity, save in one instance, wherein the funeral pyre would not ignite until it had been thrice kindled, and even then it burnt so slowly that it seemed as though, for an hour, the lambent tongues of flame would not lick around their prey.

The victim, in this case, was a beautiful young girl, scarcely eighteen years of age, with eyes blue as the summer sunshine, a complexion bright, delicate, and transparent as the petals of the China rose, with arched brows, long fringed lashes, and clustering tresses of hair black as the raven's wing, which flowed adown her milk-white back and over her rounded and dimpled shoulders in glossy, rippling waves.

The form of this young girl was of divine loveliness, perfect in its rounded contours, exquisite in the purity, the delicacy, and the softness of its skin; and yet she alone, out of the whole batch of victims, seemed to be reconciled to her fate, and prepared to meet it without a murmur.

Her rounded bosoms, white as Alpine snow, certainly throbbed with some emotion, but it seemed more to resemble excitement than fear, for her short upper lip was curled with scorn, while her tiny nostrils were contracted, and her blue eyes fairly flashed with anger, or some such kindred feeling.

By this time the flames had begun to reach the bodies of some of the victims, whose white and glossy forms commenced to writhe and twist around the stake poles in agony, while snowy arms were either waved aloft in a mad ecstacy of despair, or were pressed against their owners' glowing busts to protect still more sensitive portions of the frame from the fierce and ever-increasing heat.

All, all in vain! skin fair as the lily gradually changed to pale drab, and then grew brown, while the soft flesh quivered and shrivelled, and the sufferers' shrieks grew so terrible that the bear and the lean wolf were frightened from their lairs, and fled to escape therefrom still deeper into the recesses of the forest.

Then at last the hot and glowing flames actually touched the sufferers, and licked around their beautiful forms, enveloping them in their hideous embrace of death, and so they shrieked and writhed, and died.

Meanwhile, the most beautiful of the nine victims, she whose charms we have the most carefully depicted, stood erect and dignified against the stake to which she was bound. She had only just begun to feel the fierce heat, for her funeral pyre had ignited so tardily that the flames were yet distant from her beautiful body.

Slowly, however, they crept towards it, as though reluctant to hurt or blemish aught that was so lovely ; slowly yet surely they neared her, but ere they could change from a genial warmth to a scorching heat, a loud cry was heard issuing from the depths of the forest glade in the rear, and the next instant a dozen bearded warriors dashed through the brushwood into the midst of the astonished Druids and frightened priestesses of Diana.

With lightning rapidity, and in obedience to the commands of a tall golden-haired young chieftain, who appeared to be their leader, they scattered the blazing faggots and burning logs to the four winds, and liberated the captive from the stake.

Then uttering a glad joyous cry, she sprang forward and threw herself into her rescuer's arms, who strained her to his breast in one long and mute embrace.

Their brief transport of joy was interrupted by the clamorous voices of the Druids demanding the restoration of their victim, and threatening Divine vengeance for this act of sacrilege in rescuing one about to be offered as a sacrifice to the gods.

" Down, down with the violators of the temple ! down with the infidels and the unbelievers !" was the cry ; and the white-robed Druids and the priestesses of Diana, flourishing daggers and knives, which had hitherto been concealed in their girdles, or within the folds of their raiment, moved down upon the twelve adventurous warriors like a living flood.

Then the chieftain with the red-gold hair, that waved over his shoulders, drew his sword, and his followers quickly imitated his example.

Seeing the resolute demeanour assumed by the little band, the Druids and the priestesses thereupon paused for an instant.

Then the British chief exclaimed haughtily, " I am the Prince Cassibelan, whom ye sent to Rome as the champion of Britain, in their vaunted arena. I have fulfilled more than my mission, and have but just returned to my native shores to find that the only way ye can show gratitude is to condemn my betrothed bride to the stake."

" Thy betrothed bride had claimed the protection of Diana, and it had been accorded her, but she fulfilled not her vassalage, and the goddess, thereupon, justly claimed her as a victim. Thou hast nothing to complain of, O Prince ! and must surrender the sacrifice," answered the arch-Druid.

" If I do, may the hand that, for Britain's sake, has stricken Rome's mightiest down upon the dust of the arena, be withered to the shoulder," answered the young chief, indignantly, " for never more will it be lifted in her defence. You know me, countrymen, and that my word is my bond of honour. At the port of Itins-Portus Cæsar hath a hundred galleys, whose prows are turned towards our isle, and which, ere to-morrow's sun has set, may be breasting the waves towards its shores, laden with ten thousand of Rome's hitherto invincible warriors. Reflect, then, Druids, whether it is wise on your part, at such a time as this, to make a deadly foe of Cassibelan, Prince of the Atrèbates, when his father is on his bed of death, and can no longer wield sword or axe."

" Prince, be it as thou wilt ; nevertheless, the gods of Britain must be appeased, and, in return for the life of this maiden, thou must offer at the shrine of Jupiter the first three living prisoners thou capturest in war," said the arch-Druid, after a pause.

CHAPTER IV.
(CONTINUED.)

" Oh, Druid ! I bow to thy decree," said the Prince, reverently.

" Maiden, thou art free," said the arch-Druid, slowly and sternly ; " yet, nevertheless, thou mayest not again serve the great goddess in her temple. Return to thy father's house, solitary and alone, and reflect for three days on what thou hast lost."

" Go, dear one," whispered the young Prince Cassibelan, whom the Romans had called Glaucus. " Thy road home is not a long nor lonely one, and anon I will be with thee."

When she had departed in one direction, and a long train of priestesses, in their snowy robes, had filed off in another, the arch-Druid, turning to the Prince, said—

" My son, we must hold a special service in honour of thy return, and that we may evoke the blessing of the gods upon the approaching campaign, and foretell, by divination, how it will terminate. None must witness these mysterious rites but thyself, for verily the day will come when thou wilt be king over many nations, and a chief favourite of the gods."

According to behest, the young Briton then seated himself on a flat stone, under the shade of a beech tree, and the Druids again hastened to kindle their mysterious fire on the stone altar that stood beneath the most venerable of the surrounding oak trees.

When the flames had burnt brightly upwards, thrice did they walk in procession around the circling grove, sprinkling each oak tree with human blood as they passed ; then they returned up the centre of the grassy glade to the altar, their white robes and long flowing beards glancing spectrally in the pale moonlight, and silently prostrated themselves before it in prayer.

The mistletoe had then been scattered on the altar fire, berry by berry, and twig by twig, and thereafter the Druids had given themselves up for five minutes to silent prayer.

All this while, Prince Cassibelan, or Glaucus, as he was named at Rome, had been a mere spectator of the ceremony, but upon the priests rising from their final prayer before the altar, the arch-Druid beckoned him up to the foot thereof, and when he had humbly approached and knelt before him, roots of the selago plant were brought forward by the Eubates and beaten up in a brazen mortar, and with the juice thereof thrice did the arch-Druid anoint the eyes of the kneeling Prince.

Then a bard rushed forward, carrying in one hand a sword, and shouting—

"So the King of the Atrebates is no more, and his son, Cassibelan, reigns in his stead. Let the father's sword be again blessed, that it may achieve even more victories in the hands of the living than it has done in the hands of the dead."

The prince was shocked and grieved to hear of his father's sudden death, but he dared not show any natural emotion in so august a presence, so he merely bowed his head in sorrow, still intently regarding and listening to all that was passing.

Then the sword was given into the hand of the arch-Druid, who thrice passed the gleaming blade through the blue flames of the altar fire, muttering charm upon charm as he did so. Next he brightened the dimmed steel with the rind of the *vervain;* and lastly, holding the sword extended in his right hand, he let fall slowly on the hilt nine drops of the juice of the bruised selago.

Then he extended the charmed weapon towards the Prince, saying—

"Take thy sword, O Prince; it is consecrated unto victory. The nativities have been cast, the oracles have been questioned, the gods have spoken. A mighty armament is on the sea, and the prows of five hundred war galleys are directed towards our white cliffs. Ere three suns have risen and set, the foe will have set his brass-bound foot upon our shores, but 'tis thy task, King of the Atrebates, to drive him back again into the seething billows that only wait to swallow him up. Cassibelan, go hence, assemble thy chariots, thy horsemen, and thy foot, for a battle is speedily to be fought, in which thou wilt achieve for thyself honour, glory, and renown, and for thy country

freedom from Roman thrall and bondage. Go !"

He stretched his hand on high, and over his lofty brow and grand features there came an expression of unutterable solemnity and command. The Prince took the sword from his hand, bowed his head until his lips touched the arch-Druid's foot, then once more assuming an upright position he turned, and waving the charmed blade on high, rushed from the priestly presence into the deepest recesses of the dark and midnight forest.

CHAPTER V.

THE LANDING OF CÆSAR ON BRITAIN'S SOUTHERN COAST.

A BLUE sky and a bluer sea, whose tiny waves ripple with snowy crests beneath the rays of the midday sun, bearing upon their bosoms five hundred stately war galleys, whose masts are surmounted by the gilded eagles of Imperial Rome.

Those five hundred galleys bore an army of fifteen thousand men, and bounding in front of all like a charger smelling the battle afar off and impatient to take part in the fray, was the great war ship of the emperor himself, carrying his favourite Tenth Legion, who were clustered thickly on her decks, with the sunlight glancing on their gleaming helmets, cuirasses, greaves, brass sandals, and all their flashing accoutrements.

On the lofty poop stood Cæsar, surrounded by some of his favourite officers, all magnificently armed ; and close on the flank of his legion, which completely filled the maindeck, was Claudius Fulvius, son of the Tribune Marcus, who had so nobly won the standard a few months previously on the blood-baptised sands of the Roman arena.

How he now thirsted for the hour to come when he might carry that golden eagle in triumph over the dead bodies of Britain's best and bravest.

It was the morning of the twenty-fifth of August, B.C. 54, and the forest trees had already begun to assume their rich autumnal tints ; and, as Cæsar's galleys drew close to the shore the pleasant smell of inland vegetation and of wild flowers was borne to the invaders' nostrils.

The wind was contrary, however, and the surf ran high on the pebbly beach, and so Cæsar reluctantly gave orders for the ships to be put about ; and, heading up channel, the Armada skirted the shore in search of a beach whereon the cohorts could be safely and expeditiously landed.

This they found at a part of the coast whereon now stands Deal, and at a signal from the general's ship the five hundred armed galleys had in an instant turned their sharp prows again shoreward, and an exciting race took place between them as to which should ground her keel on the sands first.

The galleys drew too much water to admit of the invaders at once landing upon the beach, and a moment or two of hesitation followed.

It was a grand sight, a double picture of rare brilliancy and effect.

On the prow of the imperial war galley stood Julius Cæsar, erect and stern, silent and thoughtful.

The clash of martial music had suddenly ceased, and a dead silence pervaded the Roman ranks.

It was the dread calm that usually precedes the loud thunder-peal or the crashing avalanche.

Suddenly Cæsar, with one hand, raised his plumed helmet from his head, and, with the other, pointed his broad-bladed sword towards the British host.

"Soldiers of the invincible Tenth Legion," he cried aloud, in a clear ringing voice, "yonder is the foe, and 'tis your proud privilege to be the first to land and engage them ; to show what disciplined valour can effect against the ill-directed bravery of those who know nought of military tactics or war's golden rules. Land, therefore, and let your very aspect scatter these barbarians to the winds of heaven."

He ceased, and then the trumpets blared, and the great kettledrums boomed a hoarse response ; the signal to engage flew from ship to ship, and then there was a rattle of arms and an elevation of standards adown the whole line.

The great wall-like bulwarks of Cæsar's galley fell outwards and presented a wide planking stage for the soldiers to descend fifty abreast into the water, which was about waist deep, but just as the signal was given for them to do so, a wild and terrible cheer—

As though all the fiends from heaven that fell
Had pealed the banner cry of hell,

arose to heaven from the British ranks.

So horrible and terrific was it, that Rome's un-conquered legions, who had never, until that instant, quailed before a mortal foe, hesitated and grew pale, like frightened schoolboys.

In vain their officers shouted, in vain their trumpets sounded the advance, the invincible Tenth Legion was in confusion, and that before they had even left their ship or crossed swords with their barbarian, and until then, despised foes.

Cæsar was so astonished at their too evident hesitation that he could neither command nor upbraid, but Claudius Fulvius, with flashing eyes and flushed cheeks, sprang to the head of the cohort, his gleaming sword in his right hand, his eagle-mounted standard waved aloft in his left, and exclaimed in a voice of thunder—

"What, Romans ! do ye who have fought the lion in the plains of Numidia now tremble at his roar ? Behold this standard, whose eagle has never yet flown from human foe, and which has fluttered in triumph over many a red field of carnage, wherein Rome's name has become a terror to the world. Would ye see it in the hands of the enemy, and trampled beneath the feet of barbarians ? Yet that will ye behold unless ye support me, for into the midst of yonder savage horde I carry it, though not a man follow after. Claudius Fulvius, son of the Tribune Marcus, will, though all others fail, do his duty to Rome and his general."

So saying, with the bounding step of a young panther, and eyes all lighted up with the fire of heroism, Claudius sprang forward and plunged into the waves.

A thousand sparkling drops of spray flashed round him, and the tide was running out so strong that at first he could scarcely maintain his footing. Yet waist-deep in the water he waded towards the shore, never once looking back to see whether he was followed by his comrades.

But he had not left the galley more than half a dozen yards in his rear, when a great shout of triumph arose to the cloudless heavens, and animated and inspired by his example, the gallant Tenth Legion, all their old valour and ferocity again stirred up within their breasts, leaped tumultuously into the water after him, and forming in battle array therein, advanced steadily against the foe, their great oval shields strapped to their left arms, borne before them, and effectually protecting their faces from the storm of arrows that were launched at them and nearly darkened the air.

"Look out for a charge of horse—see, on our right flank !" cried Claudius, at length, to the centurion who commanded that wing of the Legion.

The warning came not a moment too soon. A large body of cavalry were coming up at a wild gallop ; a disordered mob of horsemen mounted on small, strong steeds, whose long manes and tails waved in the wind. The riders were clad in skins, all save their naked legs and arms, and wore caps of steel. No trappings adorned those fiery, untamed chargers, which seemed to snort smoke and flame from out their dilated, quivering nostrils, and to rush onwards to the battle unguided by the rein, for their riders waved both arms aloft, frequently holding a javelin in each hand, their bodies swaying from side to side with every bound of their battle steeds.

On they came, uttering war cries loud and shrill as the voices of the furies, but the Romans on the right flank of the legion faced round to receive them, presenting the points of the short spears wherewith they were armed at the advancing horse, much as the pikemen of the last century would have done, or in a similar manner to that in which British infantry to this day receive cavalry with the point of the bayonet.

The next instant the British horsemen thundered against them, but only to recoil from the row of glittering points, which they left red with the blood of their best and bravest. Again and again, however, they returned to the charge, and that with a desperate valour that won a ringing cheer even from their grim foes, but the Roman phalanx was impenetrable, and vainly they hurled their javelins into the midst of the compact array, and hacked away with their swords to sever spear heads and cleave brazen helms. As well might an army of rats have attacked one of hedgehogs, and at length the barbarian horsemen had to retire in wild confusion, leaving more than three-fourths of their number dead or wounded on the sands.

Scarcely had they retreated when a new foe was perceived moving down upon the indomitable legion, and an involuntary exclamation of surprise and admiration broke from the stern Roman soldiers at the sight ; an exclamation succeeded the next instant by murmurs of indignation and sorrow as they perceived that it was with women that they had now to contend.

On they came, at least five hundred strong, presenting a noble and beautiful front as they advanced. They seemed all to be young girls, few appearing more than twenty-five years of age, and the vast majority between eighteen and twenty. Bright and glittering helms surmounted their floating, silken, unconfined tresses, which waved freely in the wind behind them; their fair young faces and bright eyes beamed with joy and happiness, their cherry lips were wreathed in smiles, they were rushing upon death as joyously as to a bridal, for they, one and all, deemed it an incalculable privilege to be permitted to die for their country.

They were clad nearly all alike in garments of white fleecy wool, which hung gracefully on their little, well-proportioned and rounded forms. Their legs, however, from hip to ankle, were bare, as were their right arms, shoulders, neck, and bosoms, which gleamed like snow in the sunshine.

"Can we not spare them? some of those young girls are beautiful as angels, and it were a shame, indeed, to shed their blood," gasped Claudius.

"How can we?" muttered the captain of the legion, "they will attack us with the fury of demons, and will neither yield nor accept of quarter until half of them are slain. Does the hunter spare the panther or the leopard on account of their beauty? and yet they are not so fierce as these fair barbarians."

There was no time for further converse, for, striking up a wild and barbarous melody, which they accompanied by tapping their swords on their shields, the regiment of Amazons rushed forward, and flung themselves, in a panting, throbbing torrent, upon the legion, which, for once, recoiled before the headlong charge.

Recoiled, not from the want of courage or stamina, but from sheer indecision. Few of the soldiers could bring themselves to raise their swords against the beautiful cohort who had beset them, so that they at first only guarded the shower of blows with their great shields, and it was not until several had bitten the dust, and the untamed ferocity of the savages made them forget that such savages were women, that they began to return blow for blow and thrust for thrust.

Then, indeed, was the slaughter terrible, beautiful heads were shorn from swan-like throats, fair legs were cleft asunder at calf, at hip, or thigh, rounded arms, white as Parian marble, and snowy dimpled shoulders were hacked and hewed at without pity or remorse, and deep into broad fair chests and throbbing, panting bosoms, were thrust and plunged the broad-bladed Roman swords, until the very hilts thudded against soft flesh, or rasped against delicate ribs or collar-bones, the victims falling in quivering heaps to the earth.

Claudius found himself opposed first of all to a fair young beauty, with azure eyes and golden curls, upon whose lips dwelt a seraphic smile as she attacked him. So desperate was her onslaught, and so persevering her efforts to slay him, that he could only rid himself of her by striking her plump white arm so heavily with the flat of his sword as to oblige her to drop her weapon.

Then a darker beauty opposed him in turn, who, to give greater freedom to her beautiful limbs, had rushed into the battle naked, but for a cincture around her waist, though her hair was so long that it floated like a cloud around her, even to the knees.

In one hand she wielded an axe, and on her left arm was buckled a shield, with which she guarded her fair bust with great skill and dexterity.

With one stroke on this frail buckler the Roman beat her to her knees, but she was up again in an instant, and aimed a blow at his face with her axe.

Claudius guarded it with difficulty, and then with one stroke of his good sword cleft her weapon in two, and the sharp axe falling upon her little foot, caused such exquisite pain that ere she could further defend herself she was deprived of her shield and other weapons, and found her arms bound to her sides by the broad belt of her captor, who said to her kindly—

"Keep close by my side, little one, and none shall harm thee, for thou art the captive of a Roman patrician, who admires thy courage and respects thy beauty."

"Oh, Roman, I will not be thy slave. I am a British princess, and would prefer death to captivity. Strike me to the heart with thy sword, and I will die content."

"I could not hurt thee if I would, for I have not the heart to injure aught so beautiful. Neither shalt thou be my slave, for directly the battle is over, without treasure or ransom, I will return thee to thy friends," said Claudius.

She returned him a glance of gratitude and surprise, and was about to reply, when an incident occurred that drew off the young patrician's attention.

There was a noise as of galloping horses and resounding wheels in the distance, mingled with the clattering of arms and wild barbaric war cries, and presently there swept into full view a squadron of those terrible war chariots of which the Roman soldiers (notwithstanding Cæsar's vaunt in the arena, that they had conquered ten thousand of them under Ninus), stood in such awe.

The Tenth Legion would have the honour of first opposing their progress, and the Sixth and Fourth Legions were fast moving up behind them, as supports.

Then Claudius Fulvius uttered an ejaculation of surprise, for as one chariot shot ahead of the rest, and bore down upon the Legion with terrific speed, he recognised in the majestic, though youthful figure of the warrior who stood upright therein, and in his calm, noble features, and the cloud of red-gold hair that floated around his neck and shoulders, Glaucus, the British champion in the Roman arena.

And wherever the fight was thickest, the contest most stubborn and well sustained, there, like a whirlwind, swept the war chariot of Cassibelan, Prince of the Atrebates, and many of the foe fell before his single hand.

At length he and Claudius met, and the recognition was mutual.

"Away, Glaucus!" cried the Standard Bearer, "my hand would fain spare thee this day."

"Would that I could say the same, but I have taken a vow to spare none on this red field of strife. I strike to save my country and to avenge our wives and daughters, whom thy legions have slain," answered the Briton.

They then engaged in mortal strife, but the pure fire of patriotism nerved the Briton's arm, and gave him double the strength he had possessed in the Roman arena. In a few minutes Claudius was beaten to his knee, and, blinded by passion, Cassibelan would assuredly have slain him had not a lovely and nearly nude female form sprang between them, interposing her white chest and glowing bosoms to guard the Roman's body.

"Hold, my brother!" she cried; "he whom thou wouldst slay only a few minutes since saved my life, treated me with respect and courtesy, and promised directly the battle was over to let me return to my friends. Wilt thou requite good with evil!"

"Never, Stella, never! yet will I bind him a captive. Help to pull him into the chariot, and do thou jump in also, for, spite all my efforts, the day is lost, and our forces are in full retreat," was the reply.

They then dragged Claudius into the chariot, which was instantly wheeled round and driven like a whirlwind from the field whereon Briton had lost her first battle.

At a terrible pace the chariot of the British Prince Cassibelan thundered from the field, the charioteer lashing his horses to a wild gallop, and the red-haired warrior continually casting his javelins or discharging his arrows at the foremost of his pursuers.

On they went, scattering a cloud of sand around them as they sped across the beach, then up a zigzag pathway to the summit of the white-faced cliff, where a single false step on the part of the horses would have launched the whole party into eternity.

At length they arrived at a structure composed of roughly-hewn timber, with a shingled roof, over which clambered the waxen-flowered honeysuckle, and the myriad purple bells of the convolvulus.

Here the charioteer drew rein, and Cassibelan, springing to the ground, and lifting his sister tenderly out of the chariot, bade Claudius "Welcome to the homestead of a British Prince."

The Roman Standard Bearer descended from the chariot in turn, smilingly acknowledged the Prince's courtesy, and entered the building after him, wondering inwardly at all he saw, for the interior of the structure corresponded with the rude exterior, the floor being covered with rushes, and the only furniture being a few roughly-hewn benches and tables, with numerous weapons of the chase and of war, that were fastened in quaint devices around the walls.

"Doubtless, Roman, you are startled at our primitive habits in this remote land; without doubt you are surprised that a British Prince should reside in a house that one of thy centurions would scarce condescend to quarter his guard in? Yet, believe me, the voluptuousness and effeminacy of Rome is slowly undermining her power, and leading her to ruin. We copy rather the simplicity of the Spartans, with what result history will one day perchance record."

"Oh! Glaucus, apologise not to me for the want of luxury and refinement in thy dwelling, for I think as thou dost concerning such things. Rome is assuredly laying up for herself in the future tribulation and sorrow, for she is turning her men into women, and her women into spoilt children. A few years hence, instead of being the mistress of the world, she will be the prey of the Astrogoth, the Alani, or the cruel Hun. Aye! I speak truly, depend upon it," answered Claudius, sorrowfully.

At this juncture the conversation was interrupted by a wild burst of music without, and the outer door being thrown open, a Druid priest entered the apartment, extending his hands in a kind of benediction as he did so.

"Cassibelan, Prince of the Atrebates," he exclaimed, in a sonorous voice, "I come to claim the promised tribute, the first captive taken in battle, which thou wast to offer as a sacrifice to the altar of the great goddess, Diana, in the place of thy betrothed bride. This is, then, I suppose, he?"

The British prince started.

"I remind me of the promise," he said, "and this brave Roman is, indeed, the first captive that I have taken; but he is my friend, and how can Cassibelan betray one who hath drank wine and eaten salt with him?"

"The demands of the goddess are inexorable" was the stern reply.

"Had I returned a conqueror from the field instead of defeated and a fugitive, thy terms would have been less hard, oh, Druid, but my guest thou shalt not take. So I have said it, and Cassibelan will suffer death rather than break his plighted faith," answered the Briton, proudly.

"Death, then, must be thy lot, for gods rank above princes, and their will must be first obeyed. Again, I summon thee to surrender to me the Roman prisoner."

"Again thou hast my reply—Never!"

The Druid raised a silver whistle to his lips and blew it shrilly.

In reply to the summons, a wild troop of Bards and the lower order of Vates rushed into the apartment, armed with staves and long gleaming knives.

They were all clad in white raiment, and their long, uncovered locks and immense beards floated behind them in the breeze, as they dashed through the doorway.

"Druid, call off thy hounds; for, by heaven, the noble stag, when at bay, may gore some to death with his horns," exclaimed Cassibelan, seizing a ponderous axe.

"Hold! he who raises a hand against a priest of God is trebly accursed; his death, be he king or slave, shall be one of torture, and his existence in the next world one of eternal and never-ending torment," exclaimed the Druid, solemnly.

The prince's hands were palsied by his words, the battle-axe fell from them on to the rush-strewn floor, and in another instant he was pounced upon by the Vates, thrown on the ground, and securely bound with strong cords, while Claudius, who had seized the weapon dropped by his friend and protector, had to protect himself therewith from at least a score of foes.

Bravely, however, he waged the unequal fight, and down went the white-robed priests before his gleaming weapon, whose sharp heavy blade crashed through skulls as though they had been tissue paper, and cleft its downward course to brawny throats and strong collar-bones, sometimes shredding off an arm or a leg by way of change.

But what availed the brave defence against such overwhelming numbers? Claudius slew at least a dozen of his adversaries within half as many minutes, but the remainder sprang upon him like hungry wolves, and at length bore him to the earth, where, struggling and kicking still, he was bound with ropes, as had been the Prince before him, and in an instant reduced to a state of helpless captivity.

Then he heard the Prince exclaim in accents of indignation and anger—

"What, craven hounds! would ye dare to lay your hands upon my sister, too? Upon her who has this day fought for Britain and her ungrateful gods so bravely?"

"Aye, upon her as well as thee, for thy refusal to obey the behests of thy priesthood, the humble servants of thy gods, has rendered all of thy name and kin subject to the ban that will be pronounced upon them, and to the punishment that will assuredly be inflicted," said the Druid.

Claudius glanced round, and saw that the beautiful princess was also in the power of the Vates, who were roughly binding her limbs, and apparently gloating at the sight of how the strong cords tightened around hips and rounded arms.

The brave girl uttered no cry, no supplication, though the pain must have been exquisite, but she bit her lips and clenched her little fists until the crimson blood flowed.

Then all three captives were lifted on to the shoulders of their captors, and borne out through the wide portal to the sunny glade in front of the ncouth castle.

here they were laid on the grass, while three
l were hastily constructed by the Vates,
n they could be more easily borne than on
retors' broad shoulders.
place not long in being prepared, and when
morbius, Cassibelan, and his sister were
its wheach, being bound thereto by still
At l the white-robed procession wended
process the depths of the gloomy forest.
an open halt until long after sunset, the
moon h from the broad woods on to
tly of vast extent, for the
t its mild radiance over

the scene long ere its confines were described.

Then suddenly there dawned upon the startled gaze of the Roman a vast skeleton temple, consisting of hundreds of enormous stones, parallelogram in shape, ranged in a sweeping circle, and having on their summits other stones placed flat, thus forming an uninterrupted ring. Within this outer circle were still more stones forming eleven concentric lines, and at one spot, nearly in the centre, an immense rock-built altar.

Claudius knew, partly from intuition, partly from the wild tales heard in his youth, that this must be a Druid temple, and he concluded therefrom that the end of their journey was reached.

Nor was he mistaken. The white-robed cavalcade entered the sacred enclosure, and advanced right up to the rock-built altar, which was composed of stones, each one of which must have weighed at least fifty tons.

Here they prostrated themselves for a few minutes in silent worship, and then rising to their feet, the leader struck thrice with his rod of gold a flat stone that seemed as though half embedded in the grass.

To the surprise of the Roman, at the third stroke, this stone rolled back as though on concealed hinges, and revealed a black gap, leading apparently into the very bowels of the earth.

"Heavens! Surely we are not to be cast into that horrible grave?" cried Cassibelan.

"The will of the gods must be done," was the reply of the chief Druid.

The beautiful princess uttered a shrill cry of horror as her litter was first borne to the mouth of the dread subterranean passage, and she glanced down into its inky depths.

"Ah!" she cried, "'tis where the human sacrifices await the hour of their torture and death. We are indeed lost!" but as she uttered the last word consciousness mercifully forsook her.

She was then borne down the steps, her brother next followed, and lastly came Claudius, and when he had been carried below the surface of the ground the great flat block of stone fell with a dull thud above his head, and the beautiful moonlight was hidden for ever from view.

The darkness was now so deep as almost to be palpable, but it was of short duration, for fifty fiery torches flashed into sudden light, and by their lurid glow the dread subterranean march was commenced.

Down a long flight of moss-grown, wet, slimy steps, the bare-footed Vates glided noiselessly and stealthily, the light of their torches gleaming on earthen walls reeking with moisture and covered with rank fungi and black oleaginous fatty matter.

Down, down they went, until Claudius began to think the moisture-crumbling steps would never terminate, but at last a level passage was reached.

On and on, from one passage into another, across bridges of plank that seemed to span gurgling roaring torrents, whose waters were hidden from the eye, though their spray fell on the face with foul miasmic smell, up more stone steps and through holes in the earthen roof, only the next moment to descend again through other holes, and down more steps, until at last doors were visible on each side of the passage, that at this point was scarcely more than a yard in width—dark rusty iron doors, perforated with small holes near the top, and having attached thereto great locks and massive bolts and chains.

When about a hundred of these doors had been passed the procession halted, and the chief Druid waving his golden wand, three of the Vates stepped out from amongst their fellows, each one having an immense key suspended at his girdle.

Then the chief Druid pointed to three doors, each one having a door between, and said, "Open, and conduct the prisoners to the interior of their future homes."

In obedience to the mandate the keys were inserted into the respective locks, the bolts shot back, the loosened chains clanked and clashed on the wet floor, frightening a swarm of leather-winged bats from their resting places, and the three doors rolled slowly open on their rusty hinges.

Then lights were flashed into their dark interiors, revealing more holes cut out of the solid rock, capable of holding about a dozen people wedged tightly together.

Therein the earthen floor was dank and reeking, and crowded with noisome reptiles, just as it was in the passage without, while the rocky walls were covered with insects, black fungi, and slime, in a precisely similar manner, and not an article of furniture, not even a wooden bench to sit upon, or a bundle of straw whereon to repose at night, did one of them contain.

"Prisoners, behold your homes! naught is there in them to distract your attention from your coming fate, or prevent your making preparation for that future world, on the brink of which you will in a few days stand," said the chief Druid, solemnly.

"Wretch! inhuman monster! would you commit the fair form and delicate frame of my sister to such a foul dungeon?" exclaimed Cassibelan, thinking not of himself.

"Aye! what matters it? Perchance her suffering in this world will mitigate the severity of that to which she is destined in the world to come. Anyhow, her fair white flesh will in a few days be scorched, blackened, and consumed in the sacrificial fire; why, then, should a few insects and reptiles be debarred from crawling over it, and here and there, perchance, feeding on it, and sucking her warm young life-blood while it yet courses fresh and ruddy through her veins?" answered the Druid.

The lovely Princess uttered scream on scream as this cruel speech fell upon her ears, but she was unbound from her lashings, and, all half-naked as she was, thrust violently into the foul den with such force that she reeled against a sharp edge of rock, and fell wounded and bleeding to the floor.

Then the door of her dungeon was shut with a crash, and the key turned harshly in the rusted lock, the bolts shot home, and the great chain fastened, clashing and rattling into its bracket.

In like manner were Cassibelan and Claudius consigned to their respective dungeons, and then the Druids, striking up a rude and boisterous chaunt, glided away down the long passage, and presently their splashing footsteps grew faint in the distance, then their voices in turn became inaudible, and the three captives were left alone in their terrible living tombs, the only event to ponder on being their fast approaching and still more terrible fate.

CHAPTER VI.

IN WHICH CLAUDIUS FULVIUS HATCHES A PLAN OF ESCAPE.

LEFT alone in the murky darkness of his loathsome prison house, Claudius Fulvius, instead of giving way to despair, leant against one of the damp walls and pondered deeply on the situation, in the vain endeavour to hit upon some feasible plan of escape.

He then walked round the narrow confines of his cell, tapping at the walls, in the hope that his companions in captivity would hear and reply to him, for already was the solitude, silence, and darkness becoming irksome and appalling.

He forgot that an empty cell on each side separated him from those occupied by the Prince and Princess respectively; but obtaining no reply to his taps, he next hallooed, though with like ill success, for his own voice alone echoed back a reply, in the same taunting words.

Then he fell down on his knees, and prayed to Mars, the mighty God of War, to help and relieve him in the dire strait to which he was reduced.

Strengthened by this, he again sprang to his feet, and made another tour of his dungeon, cutting his hands and legs against the hard pointed rocks at every step.

Then he clambered up one that shelved more than the rest, and presented some foothold for his brass-bound sandals, groping right and left in the darkness, to the full extent of an occasionally outstretched arm, and his left hand presently encountered, instead of the hard rock, a mass of loose crumbling earth.

A cry of joy escaped him, and tearing off his steel scabbard, for he had only been deprived of his sword, not its sheath, he dug away at the one vulnerable spot in his dungeon wall, and after more than an hour's labour had bored a hole through it, so that he could feel the cold current of air rushing through the dark passage without, and hear the gurgling sound of the subterranean torrent in the distance.

It took him fully another hour to enlarge t' hole so as to admit of the passage of his ' through the aperture, but at last even th' accomplished, and, crawling through, he ? without hurt into the narrow passage ou'

He then discovered that the hole he ? through the soft substratum of soil *it* diately above his dungeon door, for i' down the outside his feet had rested*ng* upon the massive iron chain. *an,*

He therefore crept along the w at the second door, was answer the British Prince.

"I have escaped from my dungeon, O Glaucus, and I go to seek an exit from these terrible subterranean horrors. If I find one, I will return with all speed to acquaint you with my success, and doubtless we will be able to devise some means by which you and your fair sister may also be enabled to overcome the bolts, bars, and chains that now confine you," he said.

"Claudius, your words have made a hope revive in my breast, where all, but a minute ago, was icy horror and despair. Go on thy mission, and may the gods prosper thee, though much I fear that the horrors thou wilt encounter in some of these dread subterranean dens will so unnerve thee, bold soldier though thou art, that thou wilt lose thy reason, and be lured into some terrible and inevitable destruction."

"Fear not for me, Briton; my will is iron, my heart is adamant. Farewell, I will return anon. I stay but a moment to bid your fair sister also hope."

He then in turn knocked at the dungeon door in which the beauteous Stella was confined, and for five minutes cheered her to the best of his ability, with the hope that after all they might be able to evade their horrible doom.

Then quitting her, and with reluctance, for how soothing sounded a soft woman's voice in such a place, Claudius set forth alone on his tour of exploration, groping along in a darkness so terrible that he could not distinguish his hand when he held it close before his eyes.

His feet splashed on the wet, slippery floor, whereon several times his brass sandals nearly caused him to slip and fall, and as he walked on he could hear whole legions of rats or some such vermin scuddering to the right or the left out of his way, while frogs croaked, toads hissed, strange horny insects flew against his face with a harsh buzzing noise, and every now and then he would place his foot, always hastily withdrawing it, upon some cold, slimy object, which would wriggle and twist and turn under the pressure, and send an involuntary shudder to his very heart.

He had proceeded perhaps about a hundred yards or more when he kicked his foot against something hard, and picking it up it proved to be a kind of stick, large at one end, small at the other, and coated with some sweet-scented and sticky substance that resembled gum.

Presently he also trod upon something that gave out a clear metallic ring when it came in contact with his brass sandal, and picking it up his heart almost leapt within him for joy at discovering that it was a flint and steel.

With some little difficulty he struck a light, and was further overjoyed at finding that what had thought a stick was in reality a pinewood torch.

This quickly kindled, and its ruddy light penetrating the surrounding darkness he went gaily on his way.

He found himself at the foot of a flight that seemed to lead to outer air.

He bounded up the slimy steps like a young panther, sprang through the orifice, and found himself within the great rock-built temple of the previous evening.

Its imposing grandeur was still very great, though now the sunshine, instead of the pale moonlight, illumined its quaint form and the immense blocks of granite, of which it was wholly composed.

But Claudius did not feel inclined to study it in detail at such a time, and inspired by the cool fresh breeze, he briefly took his observations of surrounding objects, so that he might easily find the spot again, and then struck out in the direction that he thought would lead him the quickest to the sea shore and the camp of his countrymen, some of whom he would urge to adventure back with him to the rescue of Cassibelan and his sister,

CHAPTER VII.

THE ARCH-DRUID AND THE BRITISH KING.

LET us now change the scene to the weird abode of the arch-Druid in the depth of the grim forest of the Karlantak. Without we see only the mouth of a black cavern, rugged and wild in aspect, a large boulder at its entrance, all but preventing exit or ingress, and the bare bough of an old yew tree drooping spectrally over it, polished from the contact of many hands, who used it as a means to help swing their respective owners into or out of the cavern, and up the steep ascent that led thereto or therefrom.

Within a very different scene presents itself, for after traversing a dark and gloomy passage, and passing through a small aperture in the roof overhead, a wide natural hall is reached, with massive stalactites drooping from the roof, but the floor whereof is carpeted with the skins of beasts slain in the chase, with Persian mats, and with carpets from distant Turkey, while cushions of velvet, embroidered with gold, lie in piles here and there, and weapons of every description, the hilts and handles of some of them beautifully inlaid, adorn the walls.

On one of the piles of cushions sits an old man with a long flowing beard and a long white dress, the apples of gold that depend from each of his sleeves denoting him to be an arch-Druid, as does the *anguinum*, or serpent's egg, which adorns his breast.

He is apparently engrossed in deep thought, for he continually mutters something to himself, and nods his head sagely, and bends his bushy brows until they meet over his crooked nose, while latent fires seem to flash from his eyes.

Presently footsteps are heard without, a silver gong sounds somewhere or other, and is responded to by the arch-Druid striking with a hammer a steel shield which lies beside him.

Then, in compliance with this evident permission to enter, a tall, stalwart warrior stalks into the dimly-lighted hall, and advances towards its solitary inmate.

He is of gigantic stature and noble proportions, but his countenance is stern and unprepossessing; his fierce eyes look not straight before him, his coarse black hair grows close down upon his narrow forehead, and his thin lips seem to be ever curling in an involuntary sneer, which reveals the irregular, wolf-like teeth within.

He is clad in skins, and wears a cap of fur upon his head. His sturdy legs and arms are bare, and display sinew and muscle that swells thereon like knotted whipcord, and on his broad brown chest are depicted snakes, tattooed into the skin with blue woad.

"Great priest of the gods, I am here," he said, on entering the hall.

"May those gods protect thee, and make thee great in battle, my son," was the rejoinder. "Now tell me what can Owaheins, the arch-Druid, do to advance thy interests?"

"Owaheins may do much for me, and I may do much for Owaheins, and for the gods whose minister he is, if he so wills it," replied the warrior.

"Calenus, King of the Ragnii, is mighty; let him speak," muttered the Druid.

"Calenus might be made mightier far, were a puny rival brushed from his path."

"Speak plainly, my son, I am unused to guessing riddles."

"Well, then, the territories of Cassibelan, King of the Atrebates, join on to mine, and Cassibelan has offended the gods, therefore let him perish," was the rejoinder.

"Offended the gods, my son, how know you that?" asked the Druid, quickly.

"Nay, how I know it matters not; but thou canst not deny that he rescued a living sacrifice of the great goddess Diana from the very flames, and for that his doom should be death."

"But he hath been forgiven that crime, and hath obtained absolution," said the Druid.

"The reasons for so great a clemency must have been great, father."

"They were great and weighty reasons, be assured, my son."

"But was there no condition attached to the forgiveness?"

"Yes; he was to offer up on the altar of the goddess the first captive he took in war."

"Then the object I have in view may yet be attained. In the battle fought a short time ago Cassibelan has taken only one solitary prisoner; but that captive is a young Roman, who, when the Prince of the Atrobates went to his capital to compete in the gladiatorial sports, stood his friend, and, I believe, rescued him from death. This being so, he will treat him as an honourable captive, and will die rather than yield him up."

"But how possess you all this recent intelligence, Calenus?"

"Because I have myself come direct from the field, as the blood on my raiment might have informed you, father, and as I fled I saw Cassibelan in his chariot along with a wounded Amazon and this Roman also driving in hot haste homewards. By now he has doubtless arrived there; send

therefore, a strong force of Vates to summon him to surrender up his prisoner, and if he refuse, why he will again have brought himself under the ban, and be in our power."

"But why should we seek this brave youth's destruction?" asked the Druid.

"Because we both may profit by it. I, by joining his possessions on to my own, and becoming the King of the Atrebates as well as of the Regnii, and thou through the lands and riches that I should bestow upon the gods, were they to aid me in my designs," was the reply.

"Calenus, we understand each other," retorted the arch-Druid. "Cassibelan disposed of, and his kingdom thine, thou wilt bestow a third of thy newly-acquired lands upon the Church. Is it, or is it not a bargain?"

"The gods witness that I will," was the reply. "May I perish foully if I break my vow."

"Then I will immediately have him arrested, and unless he gives up the Roman as a sacrifice to Diana, he shall be imprisoned beneath the Temple of Minerva, he and his sister, and this Roman that thou speakest of, and there shall they remain confined until the next sacrifice of a hundred victims in the wicker figure of Ammon, which will be the day after to-morrow, at the set of the sun. Go, my son, I have said it."

So to the machinations of the arch-Druid and Calenus, King of the Regnii, was the Prince, his sister, and his friend indebted for their arrest and confinement amid the deepest and darkest of the dread subterranean dungeons.

CHAPTER VIII.

CASSIBELAN AND STELLA IN THE DEN OF MANIACS.

RETURN we now to the fortunes of the British warrior Prince and his sister, who waited long and anxiously, but in vain, for the return of Claudius.

The hapless captives now began to feel the pangs of hunger and thirst, and Stella was at last lain to rest her beauteous limbs upon a low ledge of rock, hard as was the contact with her tender flesh; and as she reclined thereon she shuddered as she now and then felt horny and clinging footed insects crawling over her arms, and legs, and body, or saw the red phosphorescent eyes of rats glaring at her out of the darkness, and only abiding the time when she would be too feeble to resist their attack, in order to consume her while yet alive.

Even now sometimes one more daring than the rest would make a dash at her white feet, scud ding back to his companions at her scream terror, but as her weakness increased from of food or rest, Stella trembled to think of would be her certain fate beneath the f these vermin.

At length, however, lights flashed in passage without, and gleamed in t eyeletholes in the dungeon doors. feet and the sound of voices were and presently a procession of bearded Druids came in sight.

They proceeded first to the cell in which the Roman had been confined, and great was their consternation upon opening wide the door to discover that it was empty.

Their attention was at last attracted to the hole in the wall above the door through which Claudius had dug his passage out, and whilst they uttered exclamations of surprise and anger, they rushed to the other two cells to discover whether the other prisoners had succeeded in making an escape in like manner.

Their delight seemed great when they found that this was not the case, and the dungeon doors were quickly thrown open, and the captives summoned to come forth.

Cassibelan and Stella needed no second command, for even instant death was preferable to being longer immured in those frightful cells.

They came out, therefore, into the passage, and Stella threw herself into her brother's arms.

"Cheer up, my beautiful and beloved sister," whispered the Prince; "we have not feared Death on the battle-field, and why should we dread him here? We can but die once."

"Oh, Cassibelan!" she responded, "I fear not death; but I dread the torture, and that assuredly we are shortly destined to suffer. Oh, Claudius, Claudius! where is he?"

"Perhaps he has escaped, and left us to our doom, for how could he aid us, even if free?"

"You wrong him, my brother, for my heart tells me that the brave Roman, rather than forsake us in that guise, would return and die with us!" said Stella, with flashing eyes.

Further conversation was interrupted by the four brawny ruffians who accompanied the Vates parting the brother and sister from each other, and marching them away, two on each side, along the devious passages, followed closely by the Vates.

At length they entered a kind of hall, wherein sat twelve old men, clad in black raiment, and these proceeded to question the priestly guardians, and to take down certain statements with stylus on long rolls of papyrus.

When this had been completed the chief of the Vates was summoned up to the foot of the platform whereupon sat the inquisitors, and there received certain whispered instructions and a key of silver, which he accepted kneeling.

Then the procession wheeled round and left the subterranean hall in the same manner in which they had entered it, again betaking themselves to the damp slimy passages without, which they traversed for a considerable distance.

They crossed the bridge of planks over the inky, foaming torrent, and at last reached the same spot where, half an hour previously, Claudius had heard the sounds of shrieks, moans, and imprecations echoing in the distance, mingled with the rattling of bars and the clank of iron chains.

The same discordant noises were still audible, and sent a thrill to the heart of the gentle Stella, and as they proceeded they grew louder and more terrible, until at last the great oval chamber, with its immense cage, full of shouting, raving, howling, and blaspheming maniacs, was presented to their horror-stricken view.

The manacled mass of writhing human misery was still seething and boiling with anger and hatred towards each other. Men hammered fierce blows on each other's faces or bodies, and women and young girls bit and scratched at each other, until their white bodies were speckled with blood.

Cassibelan frowned sternly at the revolting sight, and Stella uttered a shriek of dismay and despair, for she conjectured, and truly, that it was her hapless fate to become one of this sad and terrible confraternity.

Both she and her brother were now released from the thongs that had hitherto bound them, and, in their place, a broad ring of iron was locked around each of their waists, having a long chain of steel attached thereto.

Their guards then pointed to the cage to intimate that the interior of that horrible den would form their future prison.

Stella, notwithstanding that she had been expecting momentarily to receive this information, again shrieked aloud when it was actually imparted to her; while Cassibelan demanded haughtily by whose order it was decreed?

"By the special instructions of Owaheins, the arch-Druid," was the response.

It was useless to ask more questions, for well Cassibelan knew the power of that dread prelate, and that none would dare to act contrary to his commands.

He resigned himself, therefore, to his fate with grave dignity, and endeavoured as much as possible to calm the wild terror of his sister.

In a great measure he succeeded in doing so, and when the gate at the rear of the den was opened with the silver key, and they were thrust into its interior, it would have been difficult to have discovered whose countenance betrayed the most emotion, that of the warrior Prince or that of the fair Amazon.

The foul den entered, the most riotous of the captives were driven back into a corner, while the chains attached to the broad belts of iron that encircled the prisoners' waists were secured to two of the iron rods that traversed the cage perpendicularly from floor to roof, and then the guards hastily withdrew, and left them alone with the other captives.

The door of the cage was then locked, the procession was reformed, and, striking up a monotonous chaunt, quitted the oval chamber, the glow of their torches growing each moment more indistinct, until at last it vanished altogether.

But it was then observable that the great vault was illumined by another light, a dull red gleam that revealed one to another the dread inhabitants of the iron cage, and enabled them to hammer at and torture each other with ease.

Cassibelan could not discover from whence this strange light came, and he had soon other matters to occupy his attention, for, their animosity aroused by his sister's beauty, three raving mad women sprang towards her at once, while their frightened victim shrank up against the iron bar at her back in the vain attempt to evade their clutches and save her soft flesh from their long talons.

Two of them were promptly felled to the floor by Cassibelan, who was happily chained sufficiently close to his sister to be enabled to render assistance, but the third, advancing from quite an opposite direction, bounded to the full length of her chain, and fastened her teeth in Stella's dimpled back.

The poor girl uttered a cry of pain, and sprang in an opposite direction, but only to bring herself within reach of another crouching emale form, who fastened on to her.

In vain Stella strove to tear herself away, while the length of Cassibelan's chain would not permit of his rendering her any aid in this case.

The Amazon writhed, and trembled, and shrieked; her flesh actually quivered with the agony she was enduring, but with her little fists she rained blow after blow upon the head of her cannibal assailant, and at length thereby forced her to desist, and then Stella sank fainting upon the floor of the den.

There we will for awhile leave her, while we return to the fortunes of the Standard-Bearer.

CHAPTER XI

WHICH TREATS OF THE ADVENTURES OF CLAUDIUS FULVIUS.

Away over the wide plain, on which the morning sunlight streamed so merrily down, strode Claudius, the Roman Standard-Bearer, his whole thoughts bent upon reaching some Roman outpost, and returning with assistance to rescue his friends, Cassibelan and the beautiful Stella, from out their terrible dungeons ere it was too late.

About noon he seated himself beside a refreshing watercourse, drank some of the limpid current, and satisfied his hunger as well as he could with leaves and wild strawberries, partaking of a brief rest of about ten minutes.

He then rose to continue his journey, but had not proceeded far when he was startled by seeing two immense crows rise from amongst the underwood, and upon looking through the bushes from whence they had emerged, to catch the gleam of burnished steel.

He immediately pushed his way through the scrub, and presently came upon the dead body of a British chief, whose broad, naked breast, covered with quaint tattooed devices in blue woad, was disfigured by frightful cuts and gashes.

The dead warrior grasped a ponderous axe in his right hand, and in his broad belt gleamed a copper sword and a broad-bladed knife, while a javelin was buried deep in the gnarled trunk of an old beech tree that grew close by.

Claudius looked round for other bodies, for he could not imagine that so doughty a warrior could have been dismissed to the shades without first dispatching thither, as *avant couriers* of his approach, a few at least of his foes.

No other corpses, however, lay around, so Claudius, after surveying carefully for a moment the features of the dead Briton, so as to impress them indelibly upon his memory, despoiled him of his axe, sword, and dagger, as weapons that might be particularly useful to himself, did he chance to meet with any straggling barbarians, and he was about to take his departure when his attention was arrested by something glittering in the grass.

He strode towards it and picked it up, perceiving, though not much surprised at the discovery, that it was an apple of gold, ornamented with some chaste devices.

"The Druids have been mixed up in this matter," he muttered to himself, "but 'tis no business of mine, and the apple is of virgin gold, and worth many broad pieces."

He pocketed the spoil.

For many miles Claudius Fulvius journeyed on through the monotonous and untrodden forests, the only sounds that greeted his ears being the musical rustle of the leaves in the gentle breeze, or the song of the wild birds from branch and spray, and the only sights that met his eye being the myriad tints of the green foliage, the gorgeous colouring of the wild flowers, with an occasional patch of blue sky, when the interlacing boughs overhead grew less thick, and a passing glimpse of some wild animal as it dashed through the brushwood, alarmed or startled by his martial tread.

It was verging towards dusk when he heard another sound, rendered dull and indistinct by distance, but which, nevertheless, sent a thrill of joy into his heart. It was the murmur of the ocean, and Claudius argued from it that he could not be far distant from the Roman camp.

He hastened his steps, therefore, lest night should overtake him before he succeeded in reaching it, and before long a loud and prolonged trumpet blast convinced him that he was indeed in the proximity of Cæsar's army.

The moon was just usurping the place of the glowing sun when he got clear of the woods, and, gaining the summit of a huge bluff, he gazed upon the calm, unruffled bosom of the ocean, which stretched away before him as far as eye could reach, like a vast sea of molten silver.

CHAPTER X

AN INTERVIEW WITH CÆSAR.

The camp was soon reached, for it was scarcely a mile distant from the spot where Claudius had waged his unequal contest with the Britons, and, traversing its long lines of tented streets, the great purple-silk pavilion of the Emperor presently rose before the anxious Standard Bearer's view.

A centurion's guard was stationed in front of the looped-up curtains that formed the entrance, and these being also warriors of the Tenth Legion immediately recognised Claudius on his near approach, though the fact of their being on duty before the tent of their Emperor prevented their welcoming him, or further testifying the joy they felt at his return, than by smiles and mute signs.

"I will at once announce you, my Claudius," whispered Eumolpus, as he quitted our hero's side; and, advancing to the door of the tent, he gave the centurion on duty the necessary challenge and countersign, and was permitted to pass in.

He presently reappeared with a smiling countenance, and told Claudius that the Emperor had been about to retire to rest, but on being informed of his Standard Bearer's safety he had hastily resumed such clothing as he had already divested himself of, and expressed an intense desire to see him at once.

Claudius permitted himself, therefore, to be hurried by his friend towards the Imperial tent, and presently found himself in the presence of the Emperor.

The interior of Cæsar's pavilion was carpeted with the skins of beasts slain in the chase. At one end stood a couch covered by a counterpane of purple silk, while the white pillows were heavily fringed with gold. Near by stood a gilded chair of State, and the glittering armour and weapons used by the Emperor in battle hung from the central pole, flashing like burnished silver.

Cæsar, who had awaited the entrance of Claudius seated in the gilded chair before mentioned, rose as the Standard Bearer approached, and advanced three steps to meet him, saying :—" Claudius, we are glad that Rome has not lost a true son, and her army a strong arm and valiant heart. Welcome back to camp."

Claudius sank gracefully on one knee, and kissed the Emperor's hand.

"My eye was on you throughout the battle, Claudius," continued the Emperor ; " I saw how you so gallantly leapt from the galley, when all others wavered, and led the way, inspiring them to imitate your bravery. I saw you in the thick of the fight, and how bravely you deported yourself, and witnessed your capture by the British charioteer, and your being borne from the field a captive."

Claudius again bowed his head and kissed the Emperor's hand.

"I saw all this," continued Cæsar, "and unknown to you I have already bestowed on you a reward, one that will, I think, please you."

"My Emperor, it is one, perhaps, of which I am undeserving."

"Nay, I am the best judge of that," answered Cæsar, with a smile ; " but thou dost not ask me what the reward is. Hast thou no curiosity?"

"Patience is the soldier's best virtue. I waited for my Emperor to tell me."

"It is, then, thy father's freedom and restoration to our full favour. We cannot deem the parent of so brave a son a traitor ; we conclude, therefore, that he has been misjudged. We do not pardon, for there is nothing to forgive ; but Marcus Fulvius is again a tribune, the edict against him is annulled, and trusty messengers were despatched to Gaul an hour after thy being taken captive, to effect this, so that within a month he will be in Rome, and on our return he will clasp thee to his arms, knowing that thy bravery and devotion have done all."

Claudius Fulvius was too affected by Cæsar's noble conduct to express his gratitude in words. He merely gasped forth—

"My Emperor, I am yours and Rome's to the death. A rough soldier, I cannot return meet thanks for this great favour ; let my future deeds show my gratitude."

"I am content that they should do so," answered Cæsar. "Behold your standard in yonder corner of the tent; I would intrust its keeping to no less worthy hands. Take it again in thy strong, loyal grasp, and advance it wherever glory and Rome's honour point the way."

Claudius sprang towards the eagle-guerdoned standard with a cry of joy ; he seized its long pole with a grip of iron, and raised it above his head ; but the next instant a cloud of passing sorrow overspread his features, and, resigning it again, he returned slowly to the footstool of the Emperor's chair of state, and, prostrating himself before it, said—

"Oh ! great Cæsar, before I am again called upon to join the legion, I pray thee to let me depart upon another service, one which will take but few hours to perform, and which has for its object the releasing of a great and valiant British prince, and his lovely and heroic sister, from a bondage worse than death, from a thraldom more hideous than that of the grave."

"Explain thyself fully, my son, and I will listen," said the Emperor.

Thus urged, Claudius told Cæsar in detail the whole of his adventures, with which the reader is already acquainted, from the moment of his being taken prisoner by the British Prince

Cæsar reflected profoundly for a minute or two, and then, raising his head, he said, with a smile which had something of scorn in it—

"Claudius, thou shalt go, and shouldst thou succeed in thy enterprise let this British Prince know that he owes his own and his sister's liberty as much to Cæsar as to thee. Embitter his heart against these Druids, who have heaped upon him so great an injustice, and tempt him to seek revenge upon them by becoming *our* ally, for well I know that the Atrebates are one of the largest of the British tribes, and to win this Prince over to our banners were worth the loss of a thousand men. Go, Claudius, thy boon is granted, take with thee as many men as thou wilt, and may the gods prosper thy mission."

Again the Standard Bearer bent his head, though not without sorrow that sordid motives and self interest should be at the bottom of this act of seeming generosity. Then he sprang erect to his feet, and making a stiff military salute, retired backwards from the tent.

Without losing a moment he sought out his friend Eumolpus, and told him of the success of his petition, who, thereupon, volunteered, with the whole of his company, to join him in his backward march to the temple of Minerva, and half an hour later, forty strong, they were on the road thither.

Ah ! little did Claudius imagine that long ere this Cassibelan and Stella had been removed from their dungeons, to be confined in the still more terrible and infinitely more perilous cage of maniacs in the oval chamber.

CHAPTER IX.

AN INTERRUPTED SACRIFICE.

FOR hour after hour did the British Prince and his beauteous sister linger in momentary peril of their lives in that dreadful cage, filled with howling, raving, and struggling lunatics, the destined victims of the gods.

Cassibelan protected himself with ease from all the fierce attacks made upon him, but he was not always enabled to defend Stella, for the length of his chain would not sometimes permit of his coming within reach of those who strove artfully and stealthily to creep upon her from an opposite direction.

After this state of things had lasted for many hours, footsteps were again audible in the stone corridors without, each moment sounding nearer.

Then lights gleamed in the distance, and presently a Druid procession entered the great rocky chamber, many carrying torches.

The arch-Druid was at their head in his full vestments of office.

Behind him came the Sacerda, who were in turn followed by the Vates and the Bards, while two-score brawny and half-naked ruffians brought up the rear, each one holding a long chain in his left hand, and a stout-handled whip, with long knotted thongs, in his right hand.

The priestly portion of the procession took up its position at the lower end of the oval chamber, with the arch-Druid in front, and struck up a dull, monotonous chant, while the men armed with the whips and chains proceeded to open the doors of the iron cage, having effected which, they rushed into its interior, and proceeded to lash its inmates into a state of submission.

The cries and groans of unfortunates were drowned by the swelling chorus of the priests, which continued to wax louder and louder as the yells of pain and agony increased in intensity. The victims soon, however, grew tranquil, and then they were released from the uprights to which they had been bound, and each ruffian taking charge of two, they were driven in couples like leashed hounds out of the cage and into the centre of the rocky hall.

The procession then re-formed, and, with the Druids leading the way, marched towards the mouth of the subterranean passage, the lurid torchlight flashing on the wet walls, the boisterous chorus of the chaunting priests echoing adown long gloomy corridors and rock-hewn passages, and blending with the roar of the distant torrent in one terrible hell of sound.

Doggedly and silently in the rear, cowed into insanity and submission by the thonged lashes that descended unsparingly upon their naked backs, walked the victims of the gods, chained in couples, downcast and sullen.

Cassibelan and his sister were together, his right wrist being manacled to her left, and a great iron ring encircling each of their waists, to which were attached chains, the ends whereof were grasped by a brawny ruffian, who urged them on with the harsh crackings of his terrible whip.

As yet he had stricken with it neither of his captives, though, as the knotted thongs whizzed past Stella's ears her white shoulders would heave and her beautiful back quiver in momentary expectation of the blow, and Cassibelan would endeavour to interpose a brawny arm to protect her delicate flesh from the upraised lash.

In this way the long stone staircase leading to the trap-door was at last reached and surmounted, the door itself was rolled back, and the next minute the subterranean vaults were left behind, and the whole party stood within the great rock-built temple of Minerva, with the cool air of evening blowing refreshingly upon their faces.

"Oh! Cassibelan, is not this beautiful?" gasped Stella. "Let me breathe and die."

"Alas! my sister, would that it could be so; but this is only the beginning of the end, and our approaching deaths will be those of intense anguish and torture. Look yonder, dear Stella, and strengthen thy heart for the worst."

The lovely girl gazed in the direction in which her brother pointed with his manacled hand, and beheld, standing right in front of the rock-built altar, a colossal figure of a man, but formed of wicker-work, and fully forty feet in height, by in many places twenty in width.

The interior of this unsightly figure was hollow, and around it piles of brushwood were laid, which were seemingly sprinkled with a black pitchy substance, which gave forth a nauseous smell.

The use of this fell figure was apparent in a moment. It was an idol, into which they were all to be thrust, pell-mell, one on the top of the other, until it was full from foot to head, when it would be set on fire, and they would be consumed therein—a struggling, seething mass of humanity, without the slightest chance of escape or deliverance.

Already the two-score ruffians who had driven them from the vaults had begun their work; a great trap door in the back of the wicker-work image had been opened, short stumpy ladders had been placed against its legs, and up them the passive victims, both male and female, were being dragged, and then pitched promiscuously into the interior of the idol.

At length the moment arrived in which Cassibelan and Stella were in turn to be hurled into the capacious interior of the idol, which already contained seventy-eight writhing, moaning victims.

Four powerful ruffians approached and laid hold of them, in whose grasp, manacled as they were, they were powerless as infants.

Two of them clutched Stella's white arms with a grip that turned the snowy skin a leaden colour in an instant. The others laid hold of the brother, and away they were led in silence towards the dread image.

The ladders were now so long that Cassibelan and Stella had to ascend them in front of their guards, who accelerated their speed with cruel blows, but at last they reached the summit, and of their own accord clambered into the interior of the image, resting as lightly as possible on the bodies of those who formed their throbbing, heaving floor.

The head-covering of the idol was then replaced, a more boisterous chorus than ever broke from the Druid priesthood, and, amid the long rolling cadence of sound, torches were kindled into ruddy flame, and then plunged deep into the loose piles of brushwood that encircled the dread wicker idol, with its eighty horror-stricken human captives.

In an instant the flames leapt up around it in a vast fiery circle, and rendered the whole scene clear as though it had been mid-day.

"Stella, our last moment has nearly come," said Cassibelan, contriving in spite of his manacles to seize his sister's hand. "Can you bear your terrible doom as become a Princess of the Atrebates?"

"I can, my brother," was the calm reply. "I feel the most for the warm writhing mass of mingled beauty and valour that throbs beneath us; in another minute the flames will have caught the image, and then the shrieks of agony will be heartrending, and the smell of the charred and burning flesh of those beneath will suffocate us, ere the fire reaches so high an altitude. Oh Claudius, Claudius, where art thou?"

The last words were uttered with a convulsive sob, and as though they had been an invocation which the gods lovingly hastened to grant, scarcely had they escaped her lips than a thrilling cheer rang upwards to the midnight heavens, and a troop of Roman soldiers, in all their glittering panoply of steel and scarlet, their sword-blades and spear-heads sparkling in the ruddy light, dashed forth from the thick underwood, and at their head, fiery and impassioned as a war-god, strode Claudius Fulvius, with Eumolpus, the centurion, close behind him.

The victims who were imprisoned therein, with the exception of some half-dozen at the top, could not, however, see their approach, owing to the black wreaths of smoke that by this time whirled around the idol, and thus they guessed not that deliverance was so near at hand; but amongst those who did witness the Roman advance were Cassibelan and his sister Stella, and the latter, immediately recognising Claudius Fulvius at the head of the little band, exclaimed, in accents of joy—

"Behold, my brother—said I not that the Roman warrior would be true?"

"True as his own tried steel," responded the Prince;. "sorry am I that I doubted him for an instant; but, oh! will they yet be in time?"

Well, indeed, might this doubt arise in the Briton's heart; for the smoke-fumes had suddenly become stifling, and the groans and gasps for breath that rose to their ears from the warm quivering mass of humanity beneath them was something appalling and perfectly heart-rending to feelings less hard than adamant.

A minute longer and they would have been too late; for the immense wicker image would by that time have been ignited, and a column of flame, a hundred feet in height, would have clasped the eighty victims in its dread embrace. Even now it was blackened in parts by the fire, and the bodies of many victims which had been pressed up close against its outside ribs were scorched brown by the great heat, whilst many were suffocated outright, or crushed to death by the superincumbent weight of those above.

But the Roman soldiers were not long in tearing the idol itself in pieces, and liberating the imprisoned victims.

Then it was discovered that out of the four score sufferers forty-five had escaped with trifling hurts or bruises, twenty were so seriously injured that their ultimate recovery was a matter of doubt and uncertainty, and fifteen had found peace in death—the majority of whom had perished from suffocation, not the flames.

Claudius it was, who, planting a ladder at the back of the idol, bounded up it, and, lifting the covering from the head of the image, extended his arms to release the beauteous Stella from her frightful imprisonment.

She was still in a swoon, but he lifted her out of the idol's head as though she had been a child, and descended the ladder, bearing her in his arms with all the tenderness of a young mother.

On reaching the ground he carried her to the side of a sparkling streamlet close at hand, and laying her down on a violet-carpeted bank, he laved her neck and forehead with its refreshing waters.

She presently opened her lustrous eyes, and gazing into his with a look of deep love and trusting confidence, murmured in a low tone—

"I knew that you would come back, Claudius. I only feared that you might not arrive in time, might not return until all was over."

Then the Roman Standard-Bearer strained the beauteous British maiden to his breast in one long, mute embrace, oblivious in that moment of ecstacy of aught else in the world besides, and he was only awakened from his delicious reverie by hearing a voice at his side exclaim—

"My sister is too overcome to thank thee, oh chivalrous Roman, for this gallant rescue; let me, therefore, do so, both on her behalf and my own, and believe me that in Cassibelan, King of the Atrebates, you will find neither ingratitude for, nor forgetfulness of, the great service thou hast rendered him and his this day."

Claudius laid Stella on the grass, and grasped the hand of the King, which was extended towards him, saying with emphasis—

"I have but ratified the bond of friendship which we each swore to one another on the blood-stained sands of the Roman arena. A soldier's word and a soldier's sword are his only treasures, and they should be ever staunch and true."

As his followers were now clamouring for his presence, Claudius left Stella in charge of her brother, and returned to them.

He found that Eumolpus, the centurion, his second in command, had secured all the Druid prisoners with the ropes and chains wherewith the sacrificial victims had erst been bound.

Twelve only of their number had been slain, but many of the survivors were more or less seriously wounded, and amongst the latter was Owaheino, the arch-Druid, whose face had received a sword gash, not very deep, but sufficiently so to spoil its former expression of stern, but intellectual beauty.

Fearing that some of the escaped Britons might ere long return with reinforcements powerful enough to turn the fate of the day, and undo all that he and his cohort had effected, Claudius determined to quit the vicinity of the grim Temple of Minerva with all possible speed and despatch.

Claudius had been instructed by Cæsar to use his best endeavours to induce the British Prince Cassibelan, and he certainly used his persuasive powers as they went onwards.

For the British prince had resolved to accompany Claudius to within a reasonable distance of the Roman camp, that the standard-bearer might not lose his way.

Stella was carried on a rude litter by some of those rescued uninjured from the idol, all of whom preferred to join the fortunes of Cassibelan, and had armed themselves with weapons taken from the slain Druids and their myrmidons. Claudius was very eloquent as they marched along.

He depicted in strong colours the injuries and injustices that he had suffered at the hands of his countrymen; recalled how he and all whom he loved had been persecuted by the Druids, who were the real rulers of Britain, while the territorial kings and princes were but puppets in their hands, and he urged him to obtain vengeance upon them by allying his armies with those of Rome; when, Britain vanquished, the Emperor would bestow upon him territories of thrice the extent of those he now possessed, and perhaps even constitute him viceroy over the whole kingdom.

The British King listened patiently to his words, but when he had concluded he took his hand in his, and said, with calm dignity—

"Claudius, I am a Briton; I am a patriot, and I love my country. No matter what wrongs I suffer, therefore, from the hands of those who also call themselves Britain's sons, the air I breathe, the purple heather whereon I tread, the dark woods in which I hunt, and the bright rivers wherein I fish and bathe, have harmed me not. 'Tis them which I love, and rather than see all these heirlooms of my race under foreign yoke, I will die, sword in hand, in their defence; but to aid the invader to win them from us, though he were to bestow upon me as a reward the gilded shell of a Viceroyship!—Never!"

And Claudius saw from his manner that it was vain to urge him further.

They parted with many hopes of soon meeting again, with many regrets that untoward circumstances combined to separate them, even for a time, and with mutual assurances that each would never forget the other, and not before they had sealed the compact of their love with more than one burning kiss on lips and brow.

And now the Standard-Bearer, and his friend Eumolpus, the centurion, strode along the green forest glades some few yards ahead of their followers, conversing on a hundred different topics in turn, but chiefly upon the campaign, and the

loss of the eighteen war galleys containing the whole of Cæsar's cavalry, the news of which catastrophe had reached the camp just before they had quitted it on the preceding evening.

At length they came in sight of a human habitation, a mere hut erected rudely with timber in a little open glade, and of but one storey in height.

As they drew near unto this primitive structure, cries echoed from within, shrill cries of terror uttered in a woman's voice, and Claudius and Eumolpus, making signs to their soldiers to quickly follow, rushed forward to the rescue.

They found the door of the hut unbarred, and, softly gliding into the interior, they, whilst yet unperceived, beheld a sight that fairly riveted them to the spot.

The hut consisted of but one chamber, but that was very large and lofty. The floor was strewn with rushes, and a few articles of rudely-constructed furniture, such as stools, tables, and benches, were scattered here and there. Instruments of the chase and of warfare hung suspended against the walls, and on the hearth burned a bright fire; but the attention of the Romans was concentrated upon a couch that stood in one corner of the hut, whereon reclined a lovely British girl, crouching in an attitude of terror, while standing by her side, with the bare blade of a dagger glittering in her upraised right hand, stood another female form, evidently menacing, in a fit of furious and uncontrollable passion, her life.

The young girl on the couch had apparently retired to rest. She was very beautiful, and scarcely eighteen years of age, with eyes blue as the summer sunshine, a complexion bright, delicate, and transparent as the petals of the China rose, arched brows, long fringed lashes, and clustering tresses of hair, black as the raven's wing, which floated down her back and over her shoulders in glossy, rippling waves.

As contrasted with the stately figure of the female who stood by her bedside, she was as a lithe willow compared with a majestic oak.

She also was young, for, probably, she had not seen twenty summers, and if her victim was beautiful she was grandly handsome. The former had the features of a Venus, the latter of a Minerva, combined with the form of the hunting goddess, Diana. No lithe, swaying, undulating outlines had she, but a figure proud, erect, massive, and splendidly developed. Her arms, had they displayed ridges of muscles instead of a smooth, glossy roundness, would have been worthy of a young gladiator.

Her upraised right arm glittered like that of some beautiful statue in the firelight, and her white robes bordered with gold braid, and the coronet of gems that sparkled amid the raven tresses of her hair, disclosed the fact that she was the high priestess of Diana.

"Die, apostate wretch!" she hissed forth at her victim; "doomed a propitiatory offering to appease the wrath of the goddess, you yet dared to evade your fate. Was it not so?"

"I was saved by Prince Cassibelan," answered the trembling girl (in whom we now recognise the beauteous victim to Diana, the betrothed bride of the red-haired British Prince, whose rescue from her funeral pyre we have described in an early chapter of this romance); "yes, not only saved by him, but pardoned by the arch-Druid, who bid me go in peace."

"The promise was made under compulsion and was therefore nothing worth. The arch-Druid considered it as not binding on his conscience, and sent me word, authorising me or any of the sister-hood to slay you when and where we listed. Well, in pursuance of that authority, here I am, and your last minute of life, foul minion, has arrived."

Then she carefully pressed the point of her dagger upon a tiny spray-shaped purple vein that just covered the throbbing centre of life, and pierced the outer skin.

The young girl uttered a cry more of horror than pain, but moved not.

"That is right!" said the high priestess. "I have marked the spot for the scarcely perceptible punctured wound! I will count slowly forty-five, during which time thou canst pray; then I will thrust home with all my strength, and in an instant thou wilt be a beautiful corpse! Now!—one!—two!——"

She began to count, slowly as the tick of a pendulum, while her victim lay motionless and still, her arms crossed on her chest, her eyes raised to heaven, her lips moving in silent prayer, and her statuesque form stretched out to its full length, as though she were already a corpse and laid out for interment.

"One!—two!—three!—four!—five!" and so on the arch-priestess slowly counted; but ere she had reached the fatal number of forty-five Claudius Fulvius and Eumolpus, recovering from the stupor of mingled horror, astonishment, and admiration under which they had till then laboured, sprung forward, and, clutching the would-be murderess in no gentle grip, dragged her away from the couch and flung her on to the floor.

Eumolpus then knelt on her, for he felt no pity or consideration for this she-wolf; he forgot even that she was a woman, and dashed the dagger from her grasp with a blow on the wrist that nearly broke it.

He then tore great shreds from her flowing robes, and, twisting them into strong cords, bound her arms so tightly to her sides that the bonds cut deep into the flesh, and elicited frequent cries of pain from the sufferer.

Meanwhile Claudius Fulvius had approached the couch whereon lay the rescued girl, too agitated to speak or move. He ascertained that the puncture already made by her rival's dagger was merely a skin-deep prick, and frequently assured her that she was safe, and in the presence of friends who would fight and die for her, if need be.

Upon learning that Claudius was also a friend of Prince Cassibelan she recovered her spirits and her confidence at once, but besought to be rid of the presence of the high priestess in such piteous tones that the Standard-Bearer had to command Eumolpus to have her borne outside and lashed securely to an oak sapling, so that she might not

"Surely you are not alone in this cottage?" he then asked the young girl.

"No, my father and my brothers live here also, but they have gone out moose-hunting by moonlight, and scarcely had they departed when that vile woman crept in, dagger in hand, to slay me. Oh! you will not let her return and consummate her vengeance, will you?"

"By no means, fair maiden; but how soon do you expect your kindred to return?"

"Not for hours; not until nigh daybreak," was the sorrowful reply.

"If you have such terror of this woman, we will bear her off a captive in the midst of us, even unto the Roman camp, which is a good fifteen miles distant. There she will be kept in close confinement, and should she endeavour to escape on the way thither my soldiers shall slay her."

With this arrangement the fair barbarian appeared to be quite satisfied, and after Claudius and Eumolpus, yielding to her entreaties, had partaken of some refreshment, consisting of cold venison, black bread, and barley wine, they took their leave of her, beyond measure pleased and fascinated by her artless, unaffected manners, and great beauty, and the Standard-Bearer whispered in her ear as he knelt beside her couch on parting, to kiss her hand and say adieu, that the King of the Atrèbates was safe, and would doubtless see her ere long.

With the centurian he then quitted the hut, and again the order was given to march.

The high priestess being released from the tree to which she had been bound, was given to understand that she was a captive, and had a tramp of fifteen long miles before her. She received the information with anything but complaisance; but resistance was useless, for the Roman soldiers closed round her, and she had to move on in their midst whether she would or not.

But at last the Roman camp was reached, the out-pickets passed, the quarters of the Tenth Legion discovered, with the tent of the Emperor Cæsar pitched in its midst, to whose presence Claudius and Eumolpus immediately hurried, bearing the torn, bleeding, and now exhausted high priestess of Diana between them.

CHAPTER XII.

MASSACRE OF THE TENTH LEGION—THE EMPEROR TO THE RESCUE.

One beautiful morning the Tenth Legion was despatched to a considerable distance to forage, for the Roman camp had remained pitched so long on one spot that the whole country round for a circuit of many miles was devastated both of food fit for man and forage suitable for beast, so that each day provisions had to be sought further afield, and on this particular occasion the Legion were ordered to march more than twenty miles into the interior, where they expected to find not only some oxen and sheep, but also wheat and barley fields, that they might lay under contribution.

It was an hour after sunrise when the armed cohort set out with all their burnished arms and accoutrements glancing in the morning haze, having with them a long string of horses and mules, to carry the corn and fodder that they hoped to discover ere they returned, and empty provision bags at most of their waist-belts, which the several and respective owners hoped to be able to fill.

Claudius Fulvius was there with his standard, marching on one side of the captain of the Legion, who alone was mounted, and close behind him was Eumolpus, the centurion, sword in hand and buckler on arm.

After a six hours' march the Legion saw before them the land of promise that their scouts had told them of—a comparatively open country, with huts and houses thinly interspersed here and there, and fields of golden grain waving in the sunshine and ready for the sickle.

The lowing of oxen and bleating of sheep also greeted their ears, and by all these sights and sounds they knew that their journey was at an end.

They observed some circumspection as they marched out into the open, but no sign of life was observable around. No blue smoke curled upwards from the huts, no dogs barked a hoarse challenge to their further advance, no labourers were in the fields, no children playing in the front of the dwellings, the whole country seemed to be deserted.

The soldiers, therefore, broke their close battle array, and betook themselves to the different labours alloted them. Thus some of them started in one direction to discover and round-in the live stock, others took upon themselves the task of searching the houses, and the remainder, and by far the most considerable portion, went into the corn-field, and prepared, with their sharp sword-blades, to cut down the golden grain.

Hours passed swiftly away; herds of oxen and flocks of sheep had been collected together ready to be driven campwards, and almost as much wheat had been reaped as the long train of sumpter horses and mules were capable of carrying, when all at once the blare of tin horns and the roar of conch shells broke the stillness of the scene.

"The Britons are upon us!" halloed Claudius Fulvius, the next moment, who had clambered up on to a roof, to have a good look around. "Thousands of them are advancing from every quarter — our retreat is cut off — we are surrounded."

Then the Roman trumpets sounded the assembly, and the captain of the Legion galloped hither and thither, to get his men together, the lesser officers ably seconding his efforts, for they knew that, unless they could quickly rally together in a phalanx, they were lost.

But the men were scattered here, there, and everywhere, and within three minutes of the alarm being first given, from all points of the compass their savage foes came sweeping towards them, their naked and woad-tattooed bodies gleaming white in the setting sunbeams, their long hair streaming in the wind, with javelins, spears, swords, battle-axes, steel-spiked clubs, and pon-

derous hammers, brandished above their heads.

On they came, like vast ocean waves, meeting and converging towards one common centre. Everywhere Roman soldiers were hurrying towards the fast forming phalanx, but the barbarians were too quick for many of them, and their lives soon paid the penalty for their tardiness.

Down they went, transfixed by hurtling spears or quivering arrows, and as the opposing hosts swept over them they ere trampled into the dust beneath their myriad feet.

But lo, the phalanx was completed, the Legion had formed into a vast triangle of steel and brass, as impenetrable as though it had been a wall of iron.

Each man stood with his left foot well advanced, his head slightly bent, his immense oval shield buckled to his left arm, borne in front of him, and covering his whole body from chin to thigh, while, with his sharp, glittering sword grasped fir ly in his right hand, he menaced the foe.

Standing thus, shoulder to shoulder, the phalanx presented to their rude and barbarous foes the aspect of a wall of glittering steel and brass, and, fifty to one though they were, the onrolling waves hesitated to sweep against it.

Hesitated, but only for an instant, and then against its three sides it heavily surged, like foam-flecked billows around a rock of adamant, but only to recoil like those same waves, scattered and broken by the shock.

Heavy was the rain of descending swords, axes, clubs, and hammers, on helm and shield, but the tempered steel and brass were equal to the occasion, while the Roman swords, plunging into brawny and painted breasts, drank deeply of life's red stream.

At last, seeing that they might as well assail granite cliff, the enemy feigned a retreat, and the ruse succeeded better than the planners of it perhaps anticipated.

The captain of the Legion was a gallant but at the same time a young and impetuous soldier, and directly he perceived that the foe were flying in all directions, he rashly ordered the Legion to break their compact array and dart forward in pursuit.

The soldiers, after standing so long on the defensive, hailed this command with shouts of joy; in vain Claudius Fulvius and Eumolpus, the centurion, strove to induce their leader to recall his injudicious order, and the mischief was speedily past remedy. Furious with long restrained passions, the Romans dashed after their retreating foes at their utmost speed, until they grew breathless and almost exhausted beneath the weight of all their armour.

Then the wily foe, who, all the time, had been merely retreating with a special object, wheeled round with lightning rapidity, and ere the exhausted Romans could reform their impenetrable phalanx the barbarians were in their midst, and their fate was sealed.

Claudius Fulvius and his friend Eumolpus performed prodigies of valour, and so, in fact, did every individual soldier of the glorious Tenth

Legion, but in numbers they were not in the proportion of one to fifty, so how could they, even if demi-gods, combat successfully such overpowering forces? The thing was impossible, they could only fight and die, and fight and die they did, without asking for or accepting quarter, and more than a fourth of the entire force had perished when the clash of martial instruments echoed in the distance, and Claudius waving aloft his standard, cried—

"Rescue—rescue is at hand! Hark to the flourish of the Emperor's silver trumpets. Cæsar is close by in person, and we are saved. Fight on, my gallant comrades, for in five minutes your Emperor will be a witness of your gallantry."

Then a cheer rose up to the blue heavens, a cheer of anticipated victory, and every Roman laid about him as if the strength of a hundred giants lay in his single arm.

Now were the fortunes of the day turned in an instant. Cæsar's sudden appearance upon the field, with a legion of a thousand men at his back, had the effect of paralyzing the courage and energy of the Britons.

In vain the chieftains endeavoured to rally their crestfallen followers, even by hitting them with the flats of their swords, or by dashing forward themselves and sacrificing their own lives to show them what they should do. All was unavailing. One charge, one boisterous Roman cheer, the flourish of a thousand sword-blades in the air, and the confusion of the enemy was complete: they broke and fled in wild panic, and the armed foe pursued them until their swords were red with blood from point to hilt, and their arms were weary with smiting.

Then the recall trumpet rang shrilly forth, and the Roman soldiers, flushed with victory, quitted the pursuit, and, returning, placed themselves under their respective banners, and the homeward march was commenced.

Cæsar complimented both Claudius Fulvius and Eumolpus upon their bravery, and informed the former that that very morning he had received despatches from Sabienus in Gaul, one of which stated that our hero's father, Marcus, had returned from his banishment in the country of the Alani, and been reinstated in his office as a Roman tribune.

Claudius Fulvius was, of course, highly gratified by this intelligence, and the more so when Cæsar again assured him that the father owed his restitution to rank and favour to the gallantry of the son, and warm were the thanks that he tendered to the Emperor.

That march back to camp was to Claudius a very happy one.

* * * * * *

Arrived within about five miles of the camp on the sand, Cæsar descried a lovely vista, stretching away to the left. A perfect glade, from whose grassy carpet, green as emerald, sprang up myriads of blue bells and pale primroses, white violets and yellow cowslips. The gnarled branches of the trees met high overhead, and their foliage made a glorious canopy to this fairy dell.

Cæsar, admiring this romantic spot, told Claudius that he meant to halt there for awhile, but that the men must continue their march campwards, and he would rejoin them anon, after he had spent a tranquil half-hour in the peaceful valley.

In vain Claudius Fulvius strove to dissuade the Emperor from this step, by assuring him that hostile Britons might be lurking about the neighbourhood, who, discovering him alone, might slay him, or make him a prisoner.

Cæsar smiled proudly and disdainfully, as he replied—

"Fear not for me, Claudius. I have my good sword by my side, and I wot well that, if need be, it would keep me scathless from a dozen naked barbarians. Besides, no Briton has, for weeks, dared to show his face within nine miles of our camp, and we cannot now be distant more than a good five therefrom, so I will e'en enjoy my whim: follow you my instructions, march the men quietly to their tents, and come to my pavilion at moonrise."

There is no gainsaying the will of an Emperor, so that the Standard-Bearer promised strict compliance with Cæsar's mandates, and then, not without a shudder of apprehension, watched him wheel his proud charger round, and gallop with the speed of a Parthian horseman away from his Legion, and down the beautiful forest glade.

Thither, with the reader's permission, we will proceed to follow him.

Fastening his charger to a tree, Cæsar strode thoughtfully towards the little bubbling spring, and seated himself on a mossy bank beside it. For awhile he amused himself by throwing pebbles into the water, while his mind was busy with dreams of future conquests, reverting now and, perhaps, then, to thoughts of the brilliant ovations that Rome would bestow upon him did he but return in triumph from this campaign in Britain.

So argued and so reasoned the Emperor with himself, until he was suddenly roused from his reverie by a tall manly form issuing forth from the bushes and confronting him.

The stranger was unmistakably a Briton, for he was clad in the skin of the brown bear, and his naked legs and arms were tattooed in quaint devices with blue woad.

"Ah! a Roman, and alone! This is an auspicious meeting. Draw and defend thyself, for by the light of heaven which is now fading in the west, darkness will find only one of us alive. Draw, I say; Roman sword against British spear; Roman guile and intrigue against British blunt honesty. Thou fightest for rapine and plunder, I for home and fatherland; we will see to whom the gods will give the victory," he cried, impetuously.

Cæsar sprang to his feet, and in an instant his bare sword blade flashed in the light of the dying sun rays. He vouchsafed no reply to the Briton's vaunting challenge, but calmly stood on guard, his proud Roman eyes flashing the defiance that he scorned to utter, his lip curled in a smile of ineffable contempt and mockery.

The Briton noticed not the countenance of the Roman, and so saw not its varied displays of emotion. He gazed merely into the eyes of his foe with orbs as fiery as his own, and aimed a blow at his broad chest, which Cæsar barely parried with his sword.

That the Briton was a gallant and a skilful warrior he could not for one instant doubt, for his skill with the javelin was amazing, and he could apparently guard with it the thrusts and slashes delivered at his person as well as could the Roman with his handier and less cumbrous weapon.

At last Cæsar got tired of standing on the defensive, and again lunged fiercely out, but in doing so his foot slipped, and he came heavily to the ground.

In an instant he was on his back with the Briton's foot on his chest, and the Briton's javelin point at his throat, whilst the conqueror cried, in a voice of thunder—

"Yield thee, oh, Roman! for by thy dress and arms I perceive that thou art a leader of note, and thy friends will pay a good ransom for thee."

"That will they," answered the fallen Emperor, "for I am Julius Cæsar!"

CHAPTER XIII.

AN INTERVIEW WITH CÆSAR—AN IMPORTANT MISSION.

THE eyes of the Briton opened in astonishment as he replied to Julius Cæsar, "Ah, thou speakest truly, for now I recognise thy face. Well, I am a monarch also, even Cassibelan, King of Atrèbatium, upon whom you once bestowed a crown of green bay leaves for feats performed in thy Roman arena; to whom also you once made a promise that if I overcame the Numidian lion I should thereby win deliverance for my country from Roman thraldom. Nay, thou even saidst that if I conquered the lion I should thereby make thee feel such a respect for the people I represented that they should be thy brethren instead of thy foes. Well, I slew the lion, and where is thy promise now?"

The prostrate Emperor felt keenly this reproach —this reminding, under such peculiar circumstances, of a promise which he had never meant to keep, and which he had long forgotten

"I set no price upon your head, nor will I take a ransom. Any other Briton would perhaps have slain thee without remorse, and thought that he was doing his country's gods a service thereby; but I owe thee a debt of gratitude for the deliverance of myself and my sister from a fate still worse than death, and now it is in my power to repay it in kind. Yonder, O Emperor, is thy horse, mount quickly and ride away, for there are other Britons near at hand who may not be equally merciful—up and away, while there is yet time."

He removed his foot from off the Emperor's chest, and assisted him to rise.

Cæsar grasped his hand, saying, "I will never forget your chivalrous kindness and courtesy,

Briton. Oh, why are you not with us? Will you not leave the standard of an ungrateful country, of a bigoted priesthood, who are doing their best to compass the destruction of yourself and of all whom you love, and take service beneath the golden eagles of all-conquering Rome? If so, the highest, the proudest position may be yours. Give ear unto my words, I beseech you."

"I have done so before, when uttered by your ambassador, Claudius Fulvius, but a Briton was never yet a traitor; nor would I become so, even to change places with thee, Emperor of half the world though thou art. No, go in peace; thou fightest for renown, glory, pillage, and thy name may live in history. Cassibelan, of Atrèbatium, fights for home and fatherland, for the green graves of his sires, for the the altars of his gods."

As he spoke the Briton turned proudly away, and the Roman Emperor, seeing that it was in vain to urge him further, himself walked quickly in an opposite direction, and, mounting his horse, galloped quickly towards his camp, which within an hour he reached in safety.

* * * * * * * *

When Claudius Fulvius, grasping his sword-hacked, arrow-dinted standard, and surrounded by the few survivors of the decimated Tenth Legion, re-entered the Roman entrenched position, he was received by thunders of applause from the soldiers in camp, as were also the gallant Seventh Legion, who had arrived so opportunely to their rescue, and but for whose presence not one of the valiant Tenth would have survived to tell the tale of surprise and slaughter.

The Seventh Legion had, besides escorting their countrymen, also brought into camp all the cattle and sheep which the latter had raised, and the corn and barley which they had cut down, so that the army was well provisioned for another week.

Great uneasiness was entertained at the non-appearance of Julius Cæsar at the head of his troops, and it increased when, as hour after hour passed by, he still appeared not; but at length, just as twilight was changing into darkness, he rode into camp with a flushed face and a clouded brow, and dismounting at the door of his tent, resigned his horse to the care of a slave, and desired a man-at-arms at once to bring into his presence Claudius the Standard-Bearer.

Five minutes later our hero found himself in the presence of the great Emperor and general, who was seated at a small table writing an account of the past day's exciting events in that book which, under the name of "Cæsar's Commentaries," English boys are even now so well acquainted with.

He looked up as Claudius entered the tent, and commanded him to be seated.

For a few seconds the Emperor continued to write on; then he pushed his book impatiently aside, and said—

"Claudius, I have seen your friend Cassibelan."

The Standard-Bearer started.

Had, then, the gallant Briton, after all his outspoken devotion to his country, been conquered by ambition's promptings, and come to lay his sword at the service of the invader?

Such an idea for an instant took possession of his brain, and the Emperor, reading his thoughts as plainly as though they had been spoken words, said, with a smile—

"Cassibelan sought my presence, but not with the object thou supposest. Nay, you will be surprised to hear that, scarce three hours ago, his foot was on my breast, and his javelin at my throat; yet he released me, and bid me go my way, disdaining to take my life, and too magnanimous to accept of ransom. Faith, he is a noble fellow, and a true patriot; and I do not now wonder that you failed in inducing him to espouse our cause."

"My Emperor, I did my best, and no man can do more," answered Claudius.

"By the gods, I also did my best, but no man could have done less," laughed the Emperor. Then suddenly changing his tone, he said—

"Claudius, I want to send a trusty messenger to the courts of the different British Kings, and no one will, I think, serve my turn better than thyself.

To what monarch's court am I first to repair?"

"To Cassevelaunus, who dwells in the only fortified city in the island. It stands on the banks of a noble river, and is called *Caer Lud*, or Lud's Town. His territories are large, and I am assured that were he to join our banners he could bring five thousand armed foot and three thousand horse to augment our host."

"And how far is his capital from our camp, oh, Cæsar?" asked Claudius.

"Barely a four days' march, and he is said to be courteous, kind-hearted, and bold as a lion. The women of Londinum, for such shall I name *Caer Lud* when it is ours, are famed as the most lovely in the world, and the river which runs through this King's country and capital would enable us to have a large fleet always in safe moorings, in itself no paltry consideration."

"And when are we to set out for *Caer Lud* and the court of King Cassevelaunus?"

"At early dawn on the morrow, well armed and well mounted; and if thou succeedest in this mission, Claudius, thy honours and thy reward shall be great. But be watchful, I pray thee, and, above all things, beware of the Druid priesthood, for they are crafty as serpents, cruel as hyenas, and unprincipled as the King of Darkness himself. They are the real rulers of this island, not those who call themselves its kings. And now begone, but come to me for your parting instructions the instant the sun rises above the eastern hills."

The Emperor turned again to his "Commentaries," and the Standard-bearer bowed and withdrew, thereafter seeking out Eumolpus, to tell him the nature of the service that had been cut out for them to perform, and to have a chat over the probable adventures and incidents of the campaign.

The morning upon which Claudius Fulvius and Eumolpus, the centurion, quitted the Roman camp to undertake their march to Lud's Town,

the capital of King Cassevelaunus, was a very splendid one in early autumn.

The sky was blue and cloudless, and the joyous sunshine, piercing the thick foliage of the forest trees, shone brightly on the verdant sward, and on the myriad wild flowers that broke the monotony of its emerald hue; for in those wild woods the scarlet poppy mingled with the stately foxglove and the waxen-flowered honeysuckle in one charming labyrinthine maze of many colours.

The two Romans conversed gaily as they rode along, mounted on their proud chargers, whose arched necks, wide thin nostrils, and dark brown eyes, showed the purity of the blood which coursed within their veins.

One was white as snow, the other black as the raven's plume; their backs being unprofaned by the saddle, but covered, the one with a tiger's, the other with a leopard's skin, for riders needed not saddles or stirrups in those days, the latter appurtenance, indeed, being an invention of many years later.

At last, when the almost vertical sunbeams announced that it was noon, they came to a halt, and dismounting, picketed their horses; then, seating themselves beside a sparkling streamlet, they betook themselves to the discussion of their mid-day meal.

It consisted but of salt beef and corn cake, washed down with sour Valerian wine, but good appetites are easily pleased, and so it was with Claudius and Eumolpus.

The meal disposed of, the centurion announced his determination of indulging in an hour's nap, as the horses required a rest before they could proceed further; but, as the Standard-Bearer felt no desire to imitate his comrade's example, he determined to while away the time by a solitary stroll through the forest glades.

When Eumolpus, therefore, had thrown himself on his broad back, with his hands clasped above his head, and his heavy breathing revealed the fact that he was locked in the arms of Morphéus, Claudius arose from the violet bank whereon he had been reclining, and taking with him his spear, strolled away into the wood.

He had walked, perhaps, about half a mile, when he was startled by the flourish of a horn in the distance, and its shrill cadence was taken up by another, and yet another.

Then he thought he heard the sound of galloping hoofs, the murmur of voices, the echo of distant laughter; but presently all was silent again, and he persuaded himself that his imagination had merely been playing him a trick.

He amused himself, therefore, with plucking the gay flowers, and eating nuts and blackberries, until he was again startled by a peculiarly savage roar, and the crackling of the thick undergrowth at some little distance adown the forest vista.

Turning hastily round, he perceived a huge brown animal, larger far than a buffalo, darting across the open, and pursued by a fair, golden-haired boy, mounted on a fleet and beautiful pony, white as an apple blossom in May.

The little fellow could not have been more than twelve years of age, yet he grasped his short hunting spear with an air of courage and decision, and urged his diminutive charger after the enormous brute, with the evident intention of heading it round.

The flying moose was black and dark with sweat, barbed arrows rankled here and there in its tough hide, which was thickly speckled with mingled blood and foam.

Its great eyes rolled, its wide nostrils quivered, and its enormous tongue lolled out of its mouth as it galloped along with its horns lowered, causing the very ground to quiver beneath its tread.

Pursuer and pursued were coming straight toward the spot where Claudius stood, half concealed by the trunk of a giant oak tree; but ere they had reached it by a good two hundred yards the brave boy had darted ahead of the cumbrous moose, and, checking his pony right in its path, he poised his hunting spear to cast it at his foe.

The huge brute accepted the challenge with a snort and the sudden lowering of his horns. The spear was cast, and hit him full in the forehead, but it glanced off his thick skull, and its only effect was to stun him for a brief instant.

Perceiving the failure of his attempt to kill his great antagonist by one well-directed cast of his spear, the young hunter pressed his naked knees and calves against his pony's side, and essayed to wheel it round in time to avoid the moose's charge.

Before, however, he could effect this, the monstrous brute, with a snort and a roar, had borne down upon him.

Like lightning he drew his sword and thrust it at his enemy's broad, curly forehead; but his blade shivered to fragments, and the next instant he and his pony together were rolled over and over on the grass, though never a cry escaped the young Briton's lips.

Claudius beheld the pony's entrails gush forth from the orifices made by the moose's horns, and he saw the fierce animal, with those same yard-long horns, scarlet with gore, bound a full three dozen yards beyond its prostrate victims ere it could check its impetuous career to double round and renew the attack.

Then it wheeled round as on a pivot, and after beating up the earth for a few seconds with its hoofs, again prepared to charge down upon its foes.

The brave boy had by this time struggled to his feet, still grasping his broken sword in his hand.

He glanced round once, evidently to see whether there was any avenue of escape; but perceiving none, he folded his arms on his chest and calmly awaited the death that he knew it was impossible to avoid.

But rescue was at hand, for Claudius, perceiving his great peril, threw down his spear as a weapon in which he placed little reliance, and drawing his trusty sword rushed forward to interpose himself between the beautiful British boy and the charging moose.

The lad raised a cry of mingled surprise, admira-

tion, and joy, as he saw the mailed and glittering Roman warrior, with his majestic form, noble countenance, and martial bearing, bounding adown the glade to his assistance, but would he arrive too late ?

No, the agile Roman outran the moose, and planting himself in front of the boy, firm as a column of granite, he calmly awaited its onset, exclaiming, gaily—

"Fear not, my little hero, in an instant my steel will be in his heart ; spring aside a dozen paces to the left, for I must let the brute pass me by a good yard or more."

The boy instinctively obeyed. There was no time for further converse.

Down came the moose like a charging elephant, the ground fairly quivering under its heavy gallop.

Claudius moved not until the rugged monster was within a couple of yards of him, then he calmly, but with the rapidity of lightning, stepped aside.

The moose sped past, carrying away a portion of his mantle on its horn, but as it shot by, like a flash of fire the short broad-bladed Roman sword sank into its side until the brass hilt thudded heavily against a rib, and with an agonised bellow that might have been heard for miles the moose sank quivering in death at the Standard-Bearer's feet.

Claudius withdrew his sword from the animal's side, wiped it in the long grass, and returned it to its scabbard ; then, turning with a calm smile to the youth whose life he had saved, he said—

"You are a brave hunter, little one, and one day will, I warrant me, be a great and valiant warrior. By what name art thou called, my Ajax ?"

"My name is Ala, and I am a prince," was the reply. "My father is King Cassevelaunus."

"And what art thou doing here, so far from thy father's dominions ?" asked Claudius.

"I am on a visit to my uncle Seraptus, King of Mowern," answered the lad.

"Well, you are a noble little fellow," answered the Standard-Bearer, gazing with admiration at the white but sturdy limbs and the finely-expanded chest of the young hunter, whose simple attire consisted of a scanty bearskin, which left arms, legs, shoulders, and breast bare. The flush of health reddened his cheeks, gave fire to his eyes, and grace and animation to his mein, whilst a cloud of golden hair floated around his head and neck like a glory.

"And you are a noble and chivalrous, Roman, for you have stooped to save the life of an enemy, of one who one day may prove a terrible foe to your nation," was the boy's reply.

Claudius could not help smiling at this naïve retort, but he responded with a smile—

"Henceforth I trust we shall not be enemies, pretty youth, and you must pardon me for also hoping that neither may you ever prove a dangerous foe to my country."

"Aye, but I must, for I am a Briton, and shall one day be a King of Britons, and no invader shall ever plant his foot within my territories whilst I can grasp a sword or hurl a spear; but yet believe me that I am deeply grateful to thee for the life thou hast saved, and were thou not a Roman I could henceforth love thee as a brother. But hark to the sound of horns; here comes my uncle and all his train.

Scarcely had the boy ceased speaking when, leaping the brushwood in every direction, at least a hundred hunters, most of them mounted, dashed up towards the spot.

Exclamations of astonishment, anger, and consternation arose as the glittering armour and nodding plume of the Roman soldier caught their attention. One wilder and more savage-looking than the rest galloped towards him, and when within some half-dozen yards of his person poised his javelin in the air, preliminary to hurling it at his head.

But Ala, the Prince, sprang in front of the threatened Standard-Bearer, never thinking that his little body would, at best, only shelter a small portion of the tall Roman's muscular figure, and, brandishing his broken sword, cried at the top of his voice—

"This stranger has just saved my life at the risk of his own, and now I will protect him in turn. Hurl thy javelin, Ibn Korgia, and ere three sunsets my father shall demand thy head of thee; and the rest of you come and welcome this gallant stranger to our green woods, and behold the feat that he hath, single-handed, performed with his short sword, a feat that methinks would put to shame the courage and woodcraft of the best of you."

The little fellow pointed to the sword gash in the side of the dead moose, and the hunters, riding up to the spot, surveyed with wonder and admiration the manner in which the huge and ferocious animal had been slain. The boy quitted the side of Claudius, and enthusiastically explained the manner in which his rescuer had effected the animal's overthrow and given it its death-wound, telling them of the deadly peril in which he had stood when the Roman dashed to his assistance, and assuring them that, but for him, he would have been slain.

Claudius listened to his prattle with a well-pleased smile curling his handsome moustached upper lip, listened as if in a dream, with his arms folded on his chest; but he was presently awoke from his reverie by a hand placed heavily on his shoulder, and a gruff hoarse voice exclaiming, in tones of real or assumed heartiness—

"Roman, thou hast saved my nephew's life, and placed me thereby under an obligation that I shall find very difficult to repay. Yours is the first foeman's hand that Seraptus ever longed to clasp; give it me, for the gallant deed you have performed and the life you have saved have endeared you to my heart more than I can express."

Claudius grasped the proffered hand of the King, but as he did so he looked straight into his eyes, and beheld there dissimulation, deceit, and treachery, for the young Roman was a close reader of character, and seldom wrong in his first impressions.

He betrayed not his suspicions, however, but received the monarch's torrent of thanks with a bow and a smile, and then King Seraptus, addressing his courtiers, who had by this time gathered around them, said, with a rich flow of eloquence—

"We have near us an army of nine thousand Roman foes, but we have in our presence one Roman friend. Note well his countenance, his bearing, his armour, his cognizance, oh Britons, for henceforth to all of us, at the banquet, in the forest, in the thick of the fight, his person is to be held sacred. Do ye hear me?"

"We do. Long live the gallant Roman!" was the responding cry.

"Thy name, my son?" asked King Seraptus, in his soft, winning tones.

"Claudius Fulvius, Standard-Bearer of the Tenth Legion, at present ambassador of the Emperor Cæsar to the courts of various British Kings," answered our hero.

"And to what Royal court dost thou first repair, oh Claudius?"

"To that of King Cassevelaunus, at Caer Lud, and as an earnest of thy good will, oh mighty monarch, I will pray of thee a safe conduct through thy own dominions to the borders of the territory of thy brother, Cassevelaunus, for myself and friend."

"Assuredly it shall be given, but first thou and thy companion must return with us and partake of our rude British hospitality. Where is thy friend?"

"Lying asleep beside a stream scarce a quarter of a mile distant," answered Claudius; "I will run and arouse him, and we will spring on our steeds and return together."

"By no means," answered King Seraptus, we will all journey together to this streamlet that you speak of, for we have had enough sport to suffice for one day, and a quiet ride through the green woods will recruit our exhausted energies."

There was no gainsaying the will of a monarch, and so the whole court headed towards the spot where the sturdy centurion, Eumolpus, had been left by his companion, lying on the broad of his back, and wrapped in profound slumber.

The boy Prince, Ala, declining to mount a fresh pony that had been led up for his use, persisted in walking by the Roman's side, grasping his hand in his, and, taking advantage of an opportunity when his uncle's head was turned in another direction, he murmured in an undertone that none else could hear—

"Beware, oh, Claudius, of King Seraptus; though he is my relative, thou art my dearest friend. Know, then, that oft his smile means death, his warmest assurances of friendship are sometimes more dangerous than his direct threats."

Claudius started; he was right, then, in his estimation of the monarch's character! Well, he was in the spider's web, and escape thereout was as yet impracticable, so he merely pressed the fair boy's hand as a mute way of expressing his thanks, and stepped boldly along, anxious once more to have his comrade, Eumolpus, by his side.

But when they gained the little curve in the stream where he had left him asleep, lo! he was gone, and both the chargers as well. There were tokens of a struggle on the bank, and in one spot the velvet sward seemed to be sodden with blood, while broad footprints were observable here and there in the vicinity.

*   *   *   *   *   *   *   *

Scarcely had Claudius Fulvius strolled away down the forest glade, leaving Eumolpus the centurion asleep beside the sparkling forest streamlet, than two heads upreared themselves above the neighbouring shrubs, and peered earnestly at the slumberer.

The owners thereof were two naked Britons, whose bodies were so thickly tatooed with quaint devices in blue woad that the casual observer would never have deemed that they were nude; even their faces were marked with minute rings and circles, and on each cheek a peacock was delineated with great skill and fidelity to nature. In like manner a bull was depicted on each of their foreheads, and on their chins an eagle. They were both smoothly shaven, but their coarse luxuriant hair was long, and floated like clouds around their persons.

A narrow belt encircled each of their waists, wherein were stuck a copper sword on one side, a small axe on the other, and each grasped in his hand a short spear.

"He is out of sight now," said one, at length, "and his companion sleeps soundly; let us bind him ere he can awake, and bear him away to the Druid's cave; with his body we can ransom that of our brother, who to-morrow night is to be offered a sacrifice to the gods."

"And receive a handsome fee for the exchange as well, for the body of a foe is deemed a more grateful and acceptable offering to Mars than that of a friend," said the other.

"But how shall we prevent him doing us a mischief if he suddenly awakes?" said the first speaker, thrusting his javelin into the earth and grasping the hilt of his sword.

"We will bind his wrists and his ankles with our belts, and so gently and stealthily that his slumber shall never be broken, and when he awakes it will be to find himself powerless to resist us," answered the other, with a low chuckling laugh; "but let us lose no time."

His proposition was considered a good one, and divesting themselves of their weapons the Britons took off their belts and stole stealthily out from behind the bushes and stunted copsewood.

Warily they looked up and down the forest glade, but Claudius was by this time out of sight, and the rattle of his arms and armour had ceased to echo in the distance.

And they slept soundly till they were aroused by hundreds of armed men.

But this time they were safe. The Britons in whose midst they were proved to be Cassibelan's force, who had overtaken the Romans whilst they slept. They had resolved to halt there to give their horses breath.

CHAPTER XIV.

EUMOLPUS A PRISONER.

THE two Britons crept, with swift but noiseless footsteps, stealthily as Indians, towards the hard-breathing centurion, and presently both stood motionless, the one at his head, the other at his feet.

Each in his hand held his belt, made of raw bull's hide, each between his teeth grasped his sword by its bare blade, ready for instant use if the occasion should arise.

They communicated with each other by signs, and simultaneously they commenced, the one to bind the Roman's wrists, and the other his feet, in bonds that no human strength could have broken.

Once the centurion muttered something, and half opened his eyes, but his slumber was only momentarily disturbed, not broken, and presently he was helplessly in the power of his foes.

Then the two naked Britons gave vent to their joy in cries of triumph, and Eumolpus awoke.

He started upon seeing the woad-dyed faces of the fierce Britons bending over him, and when he discovered that his hands and feet were bound in thongs that he could not burst asunder, he cried aloud to Claudius, but no answering shout responded to his appeal.

His cries, however, alarmed his barbarian captors, who, pointing their swords at his heart, swore they would slay him if he uttered a sound or offered the least resistance.

This threat instantly reduced Eumolpus to silence, for he saw by their fierce and lowering brows that they would not hesitate an instant to carry their threat into execution, and he would be dead long ere Claudius could return to his rescue.

They placed him on his horse, one of them mounted behind him, and the other bestrode the steed of Claudius.

They rode a great distance; but before sunset Eumolpus was in the presence of a conclave of Druids, who informed him that at sunrise he and two hundred and ninety-nine other victims would be offered as a burnt offering to the British war-god, Suetovid. Then he was thrust into a narrow cell in a rock, still bound, with two armed Britons at the doorless opening to prevent his escape.

But in the dead of night these sentinels slept. Eumolpus worked away for some time till he contrived to loosen the bonds on his wrists and legs; then, taking a dagger from one of the sleeping warriors, he gave each in turn a quick, sudden thrust to the heart, and they died without a groan. Eumolpus now crept stealthily out of the cavern, and seeing his own horse tethered close by, he mounted and galloped away—whither?

CHAPTER XV

THE PALACE OF A BRITISH KING IN THE DAY OF THE CÆSARS.

GREAT was the surprise and consternation of Claudius Fulvius at finding his companion Eumolpus and the two chargers gone. The marks of a struggle on the bank made him fear the worst, and he would fain have followed the trail left by their receding hoofs, but King Seraptus would not listen to such a proposal for an instant.

"A number of our fleetest hunters shall pursue them," he said, "and doubtless within an hour they will have overtaken and returned with them to our Royal fortress, whither we will at once repair, and with wine and minstrelsy await their coming."

Claudius Fulvius saw that it would be the height of folly to decline this half invitation, half command, and therefore, after having witnessed half a dozen well mounted horsemen depart at a gallop on the trail of the two Roman chargers, he turned round and courteously intimated his readiness to accompany the suite of the King back to his castle.

Then the barbarous cavalcade at once wheeled round, but accommodating themselves to the pace of the Roman, who was on foot, they walked their horses through the sunlit forest, till after about three miles had been traversed the castle of the King rose before them.

The coarse red walls of the one storied castle, formless and void of all architectural beauties, shone in the warm light of the western sky; but ere the cavalcade reached its square portal the last segment of the sun's crimson disc sank behind the green ridge of hills from which they had descended, the long dark shadow cast by the castle-crowned rock across the wooded valley faded away, and the sombre tints of evening deepened rapidly.

At last they were close under the walls; there were but one or two outer windows, or rather loopholes, but these were all barred, and far from the ground. An iron gate closed the portal or archway, and beyond it could be seen ten or twelve naked, but woad-tattooed warriors, armed with spears, swords, and battle-axes, whose blades were of flint.

At a blast from the tin horn of King Seraptus this gate was thrown wide open, and the cavalcade rode into an oblong court-yard paved with rough stones, where, dismounting, they resigned their horses to a number of serfs, who led them away to the stables.

This yard was surrounded by doors leading into the several apartments of the King and his courtiers, and crossing the threshold of the largest of these Seraptus and his train entered what was evidently the banquetting hall.

It was a vast apartment with an earthen floor strewn with reeds, and its only furniture consisted of a long, roughly hewn deal table, and four benches that surrounded it; but against the stone walls hung shields, helms, swords, axes, spears, javelins, and every species of offensive and defensive weapon used in war and the chase.

The board was spread for supper, for on it, with some attempt at order and method, were ranged wooden platters and tin drinking-cups; and presently naked serfs bore in huge platters of roast venison and boar's head, joints of bull-beef and bear hams, while others placed on the table earthen vessels filled to the brim with cumri or metheglin.

The feast lasted for at least three hours, and all that time King Seraptus did his utmost to make Claudius feel comfortable and at his ease, but as the time flew on our hero began to feel uneasy about the non-arrival of Eumolpus the centurion, and at last he could not prevent his apprehensions from betraying themselves in his countenance. But the King assured him that no harm could happen to his friend in his dominions, and that early on the morrow, at the latest, he should be restored to him, and with this promise Claudius was obliged to be content, for he dare not insult Seraptus by leaving his presence to search for his friend himself, and even had such a thing been possible, in the darkness of a moonless night how could he hope to find him?

He, therefore, did his best to make himself agreeable to the rude British warriors by whom he was surrounded, and when the grace-cup was passed round he rose, and bidding the King and his court "good-night," suffered a young page to light him to his room.

THE sleeping-chamber allotted to Claudius, albeit it was one of the most worthy that the palace contained, was neither remarkable for its beauty nor its comfort.

Its floor was earth, strewn with rushes, its walls were rough planking, with wide interstices between, affording splendid ventilation, but conducive to cold; while the only article of furniture that the apartment contained was a broad bench, covered with the skins of animals slain in the chase, which was intended for a bedstead, and the only fixture an iron bracket, into which the Standard Bearer's attendant stuck the resinous pine-wood torch that he bore, ere he courteously bid our hero good-night, and retired, closing the door behind him.

Claudius Fulvius, on being left alone, lost no time in preparing to retire to rest. Those preparations were slight, for he merely unbraced, without divesting himself of his armour, and, loosening his sword and his dagger in their sheaths, was about to extinguish the torch, preliminary to lying down on the couch of skins, when he saw something thrust under the door.

He picked it up, and discovered it to be a roll of papyrus.

On unfolding it, the following words caught his eye, written in a youthful yet bold and well-formed hand—

"*Sleep lightly, or perchance thou wilt never wake. Thy chamber has oft been one of death.*"

There was no signature attached, nothing to show who it was who took such an interest in his welfare, but Claudius felt that it was the young Prince Ala who had thus warned him of coming danger, and if so, he had doubtless good reason for what he stated.

The Standard Bearer tore the papyrus roll into a thousand pieces, so that its possible discovery on his person should not, by any chance, implicate his unknown friend.

The young Roman stood for a few seconds irresolute, then he hastily extinguished the torch, muttering to himself, as he found himself immersed in profound darkness—

"That is better, for these gaping planks would suffer a thousand eyes to peer through them unperceived by the occupant of this chamber ; now, at all events, the advantages are equal, and while there is yet time I had better effect an escape. But how ? that is the question."

He could not see his hand before him so intense was the darkness, but he groped round the walls of his chamber, and at last discovered the door.

He opened it gently, and the next instant stood in the oblong court of the rude fortress.

All here was still as the grave, for, although it was not yet nine o'clock, the King, the court, and the whole garrison had apparently retired to rest. Opposite him stood the great outer gate of the castle, and the starlight revealed to him that no sentries kept watch and ward thereat.

Cautiously he rounded the yard, keeping under the shadow of the buildings all the way, but just before he reached the iron gates the glimmer of a light beneath a doorway that he passed, and the murmur of voices within, attracted his attention and rivetted him to the spot.

Peering through the loosely-fitting shutter, that covered the exterior of the sashless window, he saw within two persons seated at a table in earnest conversation—one on one side, one on the other, but both bending over until their faces almost touched.

Claudius immediately recognised in one King Seraptus, and in the other that monarch's favourite courtier, Ongeseric ; they were evidently in some deep discussion.

The mention of his own name in no friendly or amiable tone by the King induced Claudius to pause for an instant in his flight, and to play the character of an eavesdropper.

He could distinctly hear every word that was said, and presently he heard the King exclaim—

"Yes, had it not been for this Roman soldier by some devilish mischance or other turning up at the wrong moment, the dearest longing of my heart would have been accomplished, and the boy Ala would have been slain by the moose."

"Assuredly he would ; the chase was contrived well, and the young prince had never a suspicion that the whole court swept off on the wrong trail purposely, leaving him to pursue and combat the fierce monster alone. I knew that the boy would not shirk the contest, I knew also that his youthful strength and skill would be of no avail, and that the moose would overthrow and slay him. Things happened just as I had anticipated and hoped for, but then this Roman turned up, how and wherefore the foul fiend only knows, and spoilt everything ; and now I suppose we shall have to resort to the clumsy expedient of—of—of—"

"Of what ? speak out man, don't I pay you to speak out ? and to plot and scheme for my interests ? The boy must be got rid of somehow, and you would suggest—"

"That he be strangled in his sleep : for blood tells tales, and sometimes crys aloud to the gods for vengeance, and a purple ring on a white throat is easily hidden from the eyes of the curious. This done, oh King ! and thou wilt be heir presumptive to thy brother's dominions, whose court we will visit with the sad intelligence of his beloved child having died in his sleep, and then I will undertake, for a consideration, to shorten his mourning by sending him to rejoin that child in heaven. Ah ! ah ! a dozen drops of aquetta, dropped stealthily into a cup of metheglin or of cumri, will soon release the drinker from all the cares and troubles of this life, and the next draught he quaffs will be the nectar of the gods."

"Clever Ongeseric, thy wisdom is profound, and thy advice is good," replied the King ; "the young Prince shall be strangled by thee this very night. The Roman also must be slain, for he is bound for my brother's court, and it is not to our interest that he ever arrives there. Will you be answerable for his life also, my trusty friend and councillor ?"

"Aye, that will I, three inches of cold steel shall silence him for ever ; have no anxiety about him I prithee ; but the boy first, the boy first," answered the courtier.

"You know the room that the Prince occupies ?" questioned the King.

"Yes ; the third on the left, there is a deep axe-dint in the door," answered Ongeseric.

"Then good-night ; there is nothing further left for us to discuss. I am wearied and sleepy, when we meet in the morning, and thou tellest me that thou hast succeeded in both the tasks cut out for thee, thy reward shall be beyond thy fondest imagining," said the King, as he rose to his feet and prepared to leave the room.

Then Claudius darted away from the window, but he did not attempt now to escape from the fortress. No, he retraced his steps quickly by the way he had come, and presently regained the room which he had just quitted.

There, in the almost palpable darkness, he crossed his arms on his chest, muttering—"They seek to slay the young Prince, do they ! Well, I will stay and defend him, my solitary arm opposed to a hundred, my blunt honesty of purpose against their guile, chicanery, and ruthless cruelty. Well, we shall see which the gods will favour."

He drew his sword from its scabbard as he spoke, and grimly passed his thumb down its keen edge, then he groped once more out of his room into the passage beyond, repeating to himself as he proceeded down it, his hand on the wall all the way.

"The third door on the left, with a deep axe-dint in it ; aye, I remember the description well ; Mars grant that I may discover it in time to save Ala's life."

On, and still on, through the dark passages crept Claudius Fulvius, feeling for the door branded with a deep axe dint, but for a long while not finding it.

The blackness of night was so dense as almost to be palpable, yet with his drawn sword in his right hand he never faltered in his determination to discover Ala and to save him.

Would he be too late? that was his only dread; for of the desperate nature of the probable encounter, one sword, perhaps, opposed to a hundred, the bold Roman wrecked not.

At last he did discover a door with a deep fissure traversing it transversely.

He essayed to open it, and finding that it was unlocked, he noiselessly entered.

Crossing the room to the spot where a faint streak of moonlight penetrating a long slit in the outer wall revealed to him a rough bedstead covered with skins, he discovered that its inmate was indeed Ala, sleeping the sleep of the innocent and the unconscience-stricken.

"Who is it speaks?" said the boy Prince, as, suddenly awaking, he sat up on his couch.

"I, Claudius Fulvius, the Roman. Not a quarter of an hour ago I heard your uncle Seraptus, in secret council with his chamberlain, instruct him to slay you in your sleep, in order that he might become heir presumptive to your father's dominions. Nay, his villainy did not end here, for from what they said I gathered that they contemplated proceeding to your father's court with the news of your decease, and poisoning him secretly by mixing aquetta with his food," whispered the Standard-Bearer.

"But my uncle has been very kind to me; oh, so kind!" replied Ala, with emotion.

"'Twas only to conceal his inner hate. This very day the great hunt was got up for thy destruction; and when the giant moose broke cover the whole court galloped purposely in a wrong direction, leaving thee to pursue it alone, in order that the fierce beast should slay thee; I heard Seraptus affirm this!"

"Now I believe thee, Roman, for I have been sore puzzled to account for so experienced a hunter as my uncle speeding away on the wrong track, followed by his whole court, when the moose's course was so plainly shown by his hoof-prints and the broken undergrowth. And so thou hast interposed a second time to save me; thou, an enemy of my kindred and of my country?"

"But not of thee, Ala; dost thou know well the ins and outs of this stronghold of thy uncle?"

"Every nook and corner, and every inch of the country round, to boot," answered the boy-Prince.

"Then we must be gone at once," said the Roman; "spring up, Ala, and be the guide."

The boy was about to comply with the Standard Bearer's behest when a stealthy footstep was heard in the passage without, and the door was evidently being pushed slowly open.

"Hist," said Claudius in a whisper, "the Chamberlain comes before his time, but happily he is alone; pretend to sleep, and quail not even when his dagger is raised on high to stab thee,

for at that moment he shall die by my hand. He must fall without a cry or a groan!"

He crouched in the deep shadow behind the head of the couch as he spoke, and Ala turned over on his side, and with his arms folded on his chest pretended to be sound asleep.

Then noiselessly, stealthily, and with bare feet, a tall stalwart form was seen to enter the room; carefully avoiding the long streak of light cast by the moon, through the narrow slit in the wall, upon the floor, it crept in crouching attitude towards the bed of skins whereon the boy-Prince lay.

As the assassin drew near, in spite of his face being blackened, Claudius recognised the chamberlain of King Seraptus, in whose right hand gleamed the long blade of a dagger.

Presently he reached the couch, and bending over it regarded for a moment the calm face of Ala, ere he raised his murderous weapon aloft preparatory to plunging it into his body.

"Ah!" he muttered, "the lad sleeps, and the accomplishment of my task will be an easy one; after the son the father, and then Seraptus will be King of Caer Lud, and I shall be the first noble in his dominions."

He chuckled to himself as he uttered this half-mental soliloquy, then bending well over the couch he gently felt with his left hand for the region of the boy's heart, and the next instant had raised his gleaming poignard with the intention of sheathing it to its very hilt in the Prince's body.

Even at this trying crisis Ala's presence of mind never forsook him for an instant; he had faith in the promise of Claudius, and he neither quailed, nor did any quickened beating of the heart betray him.

But before that uplifted blade could descend the Standard Bearer's sword whizzed through the air, and the chamberlain's head, sliced from off his throat like a ripe melon, rolled along the floor, while, catching the body before it could fall, and thus perhaps create an alarm, Claudius laid it gently on the ground, and said in a whisper—

"Now, Ala, let us away with all speed."

The Prince sprang from off his couch on to the floor, but stepping on the fallen dagger of the chamberlain, he cut his foot, and the sudden shock and sharp pain caused him to fall.

The rattle of his sword evidently alarmed some-one outside, for a head was thrust through the doorway, and a voice exclaimed, "Now then, bungler, is not the deed yet done?"

"It is my uncle Seraptus, by Mars I will slay him!" cried Ala, springing towards the door.

Then the clash of steel on steel resounded in the passage, and the King's voice calling lustily for his guards. Thereupon Claudius, in turn, bounded out of the room, and gaining the corridor he interposed himself between Seraptus and Ala, threatening the former unless he were silent that he would stab him to the heart, and so seal his lips for ever.

But the King still continued to bawl and shout, and already footsteps and the clash of arms echoed in the distance, betokening that others were rushing towards the scene of strife.

No time was, therefore, to be lost; and with one dexterous stroke, dashing the King's sword from his hand, Claudius stunned him by a blow over the skull with the flat of his heavy weapon, and turning once more to Ala, said, "Now then, my little Ajax, lead the way; 'tis death to linger here."

Scarcely had he uttered the words when the great folding doors at the end of the corridor were thrown open, and fierce tattooed warriors, brandishing swords and torches, came pouring down the passage, and catching sight of the fugitives, darted after them with loud cries.

The light of their pine-wood flambeaux enabled Claudius and the Prince, however, plainly to see the way before them, and they sped along through passage and corridor, until, through another door, which was providentially open, they reached the oblong-shaped inner yard of the fortress.

"Come along, brave Roman, I know a path by which we may escape, and 'twill not take us five minutes to reach it. On—on, before our retreat is cut off."

He ran forward as he spoke, and Claudius followed close in his rear, while a crowd of Britons, issuing forth from the great gateway, followed in pursuit with cries of rage and vengeance, firing arrows as they ran, which whizzed past the fugitives at every step.

At last Ala, whose foot was bleeding, muttered—

"Thank Heaven, yonder is the old oak tree spanning the ravine, had it been a hundred yards further distant my strength must have given way. Once let us reach that, and perchance we may be able to break down the bridge behind us."

He now ran with difficulty, for the knife of the chamberlain had cut his foot open nearly to the bone, and the rough ground they were traversing caused him acute agony; the foe, therefore, gained upon them rapidly, and uttered loud cheers as they perceived that they were doing so.

But Ala was game to the back-bone, and put on spurt after spurt, until the old oak tree that he had spoken of was reached, forming a narrow, slippery, and perilous bridge across a deep ravine, to the opposite bank.

This ravine was a fissure in the rocks of about fifty feet in width and at least a hundred in depth, and at the bottom of the black narrow gorge flowed a roaring cataract, whose white foaming waters could scarcely be seen amidst the gloom as they swept between and over the sharp jagged rocks.

It was evident that the other end of this frail bridge scarcely rested on the opposite edge of the cliff, much of which had crumbled away from beneath it, and fallen into the chasm below.

Claudius felt, therefore, that it was almost as perilous to attempt a passage as to stand and engage the score of Britons who were following them like sleuth-hounds, and thirsting for their blood.

Ala, however, affirmed hurriedly that he had traversed it a hundred times, so Claudius yielded,

with a smile, to his entreaties, and bounding lightly along it across the chasm they the next instant stood upon the opposite cliff and faced round upon their pursuers.

Evidently the only chance now of saving his own and Ala's life was by dislodging his end of the felled oak from the edge of the cliff whereon it rested, and suffering it to fall into the abyss.

Behind him was a huge stone boulder, weighing at least a hundredweight; he dropped his sword and picked it up, hurling it with all his force down upon the rotten and crumbling tree trunk. Then there was a momentary crash, a good twelve inches of the top of the cliff gave way, and the ponderous oak trunk fell with it to the bottom of the ravine.

Claudius uttered a cry of triumph, the baffled Britons one of anger and despair; they discharged a cloud of feathered shafts on the Roman, many of which rattled on his armour, a few even ripping up his clothing or his flesh, but he had effectually barred all pursuit, and brandishing his sword for an instant in defiance, he fled from so dangerous a position, and hurried down the forest glade to rejoin Ala on the bank of the stream.

CHAPTER XVI.

AN ENCOUNTER WITH CASSIBELAN AND STELLA.

HE found the boy-Prince with his wounded foot neatly bandaged up, about to return to the contested bridge to see how he fared, and if need be to help him against his foes.

He seemed rejoiced at beholding Claudius unwounded before him, and expressed his joy at the repulse of the Britons and the destruction of the bridge.

"Our pursuers will have to take a circuit of at least twelve miles before they can reach us," he said, "and I know of a hundred hiding-places that we could discover before then."

"Then we may rest awhile," answered the Standard-Bearer; "are you not hungry, Ala?"

"As a hunter," was the reply; "but whereon can we feed?—for we have neither bow nor javelin, wherewith to shoot a bird or slay a moose, a deer, or a bull."

"Not being able to procure what we would like, we must e'en be content with what we can get," answered Claudius, "and make a meal on mushrooms, hazel-nuts, and blackberries."

"I know where we can procure all three in abundance; let me get them," said the Prince.

"No, Ala, you must nurse your cut foot as much as possible. I saw mushrooms, nuts, and blackberries as I sped down the glade, and will return in five minutes with more than will suffice for our wants. Stay you here and lie down, for in that position you will rest better."

He left Ala's side as he spoke, and strode swiftly down a beautiful glade that was perfectly carpeted with wild flowers and musical with the song of the nightingale. He was soon out of sight of Ala, and was presently busy plucking the wherewithal for a hearty, if not a substantial repast, when a noise of wheels caused him to start, and glancing round he beheld a great war-chariot reined up almost at his side, with its foam-flecked, snorting chargers, and all its burnished brasswork and the scythe-blades attached to its wheels flashing in the moonlight, containing two stately forms. One of them grasped the reins, whilst the other, who was richly armed, brandished aloft a formidable spear.

"Ah! one of the accursed invaders, and so far inland as this! Now, by the gods, he must be some spying emissary of Cæsar, and he shall die the death," exclaimed the tallest warrior.

He sprang from the chariot as he spoke, and rushed upon Claudius, who had barely time to draw his sword and parry the home thrust of the Briton's spear.

He did so, however, successfully, cutting off the pointed head with one slashing blow.

The warrior threw away the now useless weapon, but plucking a heavy battle-axe from his broad belt, he pressed the Roman with blow on blow so energetically and so skilfully that he had time for naught but to guard and parry, and could return neither cut nor thrust with his own more deadly weapon; and thus was he beaten back, inch by inch, into the forest.

Whether it was that he had been weakened by his previous contests, or whether the Briton's skill, strength, and prowess were superior to his own, Claudius knew not; but he was nevertheless aware that he had fully met his match, and when five minutes had elapsed and he was beaten on to his knee, his trusty sword dashed from his grasp, and the broad battle-axe of his opponent raised gleaming above his head, he was also aware that he had met his conqueror.

"Dost thou beg life at my hands?" asked the Briton, in a rich but deep-toned voice.

"Never begged I life of any man, nor will I begin now," responded the Standard-Bearer; "strike, if you will, and thou shalt see that a Roman soldier can die without blenching."

"Fain would I spare thee, gallant stranger, and yet I dare not. Men may admire the courage, the generosity, the nobility of the lion; yet when the fierce beast invades their homesteads and overruns their country, in which they have settled, it is their duty to slay him; therefore, Roman, lion though thou art, this instant is thy last on earth. Die!"

But ere the axe could descend another form glided in between the conquering Briton and his victim, a form exquisite in its symmetry, and though armed with helm of burnished brass, shield of steel, and sandals of copper, unmistakably that of a woman.

The spot where they had fought was in deep shadow, but one moonlight ray, darting down through a rift in the dark green foliage high overhead, shone on a face of spiritual beauty, on a cloud of golden hair that rippled in waves from under her bright morion and over her white neck and snowy shoulders even to below her waist, and on an arm rounded as that of a marble Venus, which was interposed between the warrior's battle-axe and the Roman's undefended head.

"Stella!" exclaimed Claudius, as he recognised the features of his beautiful interceder.

"Aye, and Cassibelan," was the reply; "my brother, had I not recognised his voice, and springing out of the chariot, have flown to the rescue, you would have committed an act for which afterwards you would have been right sorry; do I not speak truly?"

"Yes," answered the red-haired chief, throwing aside his huge axe and grasping the hand of Claudius with a friendly grip, such as a brown bear might have bestowed; "yes, that should I. But why did you not tell me your name, Claudius? Were you afraid that I should not have held my hand?"

"By the gods, noble Cassibelan, I recognised you not. So sudden and unexpected was your attack, and so quickly was I beaten back out of the moonlit glade into this dark dell, that I have not once caught a good glance at your face. I am glad it is so, for I would not that two warriors in this isle called Britain should be capable of overcoming me."

"Take care that there are not two score," answered the King of Atrèbatium, somewhat angrily, for he felt hurt at the prowess or the courage of his countrymen being undervalued. "Yet rejoiced am I that Stella recognised you in time to rescue you from the death, for, by Belus, I would as soon have slain a brother. Give me thine hand, old friend, once more."

Claudius sprang to his feet and grasped the hand of the British King. He then took the little white palm of Stella within his own, saying—

"Twice, dear Princess, have you interposed between me and death. Oh! what can I do to convince you of my deep gratitude?"

"The same number of times, oh, Claudius, have you saved me from death; but the debt of gratitude I owe to thee is deeper far than the one which you can owe to me, for you have saved me on both occasions at imminent peril to your own life, whereas no dangers have threatened me in what I have done for your sake!" answered Stella, with a smile.

"A truce to this bandying of compliments and thanks," said Cassibelan; "the heart should always feel more deeply than the lips can utter; but tell us how you come to be so far inland, my Claudius, so many miles distant from Cæsar's camp and your brave companions in arms?"

Then the Standard-Bearer informed the British king how he and his friend, Eumolpus, had been despatched by the Emperor as ambassadors to the courts of the different sovereigns of Britain; how he had saved the life of Prince Ala from the moose, and had then fallen in with the court of King Seraptus; how, on returning to the bank of the river, he had found his companion missing, and had been prevailed on to stay at the fortress of Seraptus, until his messengers had found the centurion and brought him to the castle, and lastly, how he had foiled the King Seraptus in his attempt upon his nephew's life, and had helped Prince Ala to escape from his uncle's court, with all the details of the pursuit, and of how he had hurled a dozen of the pursuers into the ravine.

"Well done, Claudius," exclaimed Cassibelan, when the Roman had concluded his narrative;

"thou hast acted the part of a good and gallant man. I know the brave King, Cassivelaunus, and his young son well. Where is the boy now?"

"Resting beside a stream, not three hundred yards distant," answered Claudius, "let us return to him, for he will be alarmed at my absence."

"Good! so we will; but what do you propose doing with the boy?" asked Cassibelan.

"Why, as I am bound direct to the court of his father, I thought of taking him with me."

"Not a bad idea, and he would ensure you a cordial greeting," smiled the Briton. "But bethink you, you would be surrounded by snares, ambuscades, and dangers, for much of the distance; for you will have to traverse the territories of this treacherous uncle for a good forty-five miles, and the son of a powerful monarch should, for the sake of the country that he may one day be called upon to reign over, be exposed to as few perils as possible. Now I also am proceeding direct to the court of Caer Lud, but with a thousand horsemen and two thousand foot at my back; therefore would it not be better for the young Prince to journey with me?"

"Could we not all travel in company?" asked Claudius, with a glance at Stella.

"No, brave Roman," answered Cassibelan, decisively, "that could we not, because we travel on two different missions. Thou goest to King Cassivelaunus to urge him to become an ally of your Emperor; I, to stir him up to resist Roman aggression unto the death. Were we to travel together, bent as we are upon two such diverse objects, Cassivelaunus, the most suspicious of monarchs, would doubt us both, or at the least suspect some intrigue."

"But, my brother, picture the danger that will beset our friend, if he travels alone," said the beauteous Stella, with an appealing glance directed at her stern brother.

"His own good sword will protect him from foes in the front, and our advancing array will shield him from all pursuit in the rear. I will give him a swift horse, which none other in the kingdom can overtake, and a safe conduct under my own hand, which few will dare to violate," answered Cassibelan. "The gods must provide for the rest."

"Thanks, noble Cassibelan," answered Claudius. "You promise so much that the gods will have little left to aid me in. But see, here is the streamlet, and the boy, Ala."

Ala was sitting by the brink of the murmuring river when Claudius, Cassibelan, and Stella reached the bank.

He turned on hearing their footsteps, and started on perceiving strangers.

Claudius, approaching, patted him on the head, observing, with a smile—

"Ala, I have brought you new friends and a protector, a powerful and noble British King and his sister. This is Cassibelan, of Atrebatium, and the Princess Stella."

The boy Prince rose to his feet, and, sinking gracefully on one knee, kissed Stella's hand. He then rose and grasped that of her brother, exclaiming—

"This meeting, oh, Cassibelan, is a right welcome one; not, however, that I need any better protector than this brave Roman, who has twice saved my life in twenty-four hours."

Cassibelan provided Claudius with a horse and directed him as to the course he must follow.

The Standard-Bearer kissed the hand of the beauteous Stella, as he whispered to her farewell; and as he did so, their eyes met in one burning glance of love.

He then grasped the hand of her brother in a warm and hearty clasp, and taking that of Ala, in turn, held it for a minute in silence.

"Good-bye," said the fair boy; "a day since, had I been told that I should ever live to regard a Roman otherwise than with hatred I should have struck the speaker across the mouth, and have called him a liar; but yet this seeming impossibility has happened."

"To-day we hate what to-morrow we love, to-day we love what to-morrow we hate. So says a great Roman poet, and he speaks truly," answered Claudius; "farewell, Ala."

"Farewell, my protector, my preserver—farewell till we again meet," was the reply.

Claudius, then wreathing his left hand in the black steed's mane, leapt lightly on to its back, and waving his hand in adieu, galloped down the forest glade, and the next instant was lost to view amid a dense oak grove.

Claudius was guided in his course by the sun, which hour after hour rose higher in the blue heavens, until from its perpendicular rays he at last concluded that it must be noon.

Another hour and he would draw rein, and, dismounting, give his good horse a rest, while he searched for some fruit and berries wherewith to satisfy his own hunger, and thereafter, perhaps, take an hour's slumber in some secluded glade.

Warned by the fate of Eumolpus on the preceding day he resolved not to camp in the open, or by the side of the stream, lest some wary Britons might catch him napping and kill him, or take him prisoner, before he was aware of their presence.

These thoughts made him more cautious in the present too, and he rode more circumspectly; yet, before he had proceeded much farther, an arrow sped from out a thicket on his right, and shivered to fragments on his helmet of proof.

Another and another followed, but they were all caught either on his shield, helm or breastplate, and before any more could be discharged he had leaped his black charger right over the breast-high brushwood into the midst of an ambuscade of more than a dozen armed Britons, upon whom he came like a descending thunderbolt.

Down they cast their bows, and handled spear, sword, and battle-axe in their place.

In an instant a hundred bare blades were raised on high to cut him down, but ere a single one of them could descend another shadowy form on horseback darted in amid the host, exclaiming in tones of thunder—

" Hold out, Claudius ; a hundred of our horse-soldiers are but half a mile in our rear. Hack, hew, and spare not ; we will soon scatter this rabble rout to the four winds of Heaven. Here, take my axe."

The new arrival thrust the iron handle of an axe into the Standard-Bearer's hand, striking to right and left with his good sword as he did so.

He soon cleared a wide ring around Claudius and at every blow he dealt, he kept crying—

" Wait until our other horsemen come, you rascals, and we will massacre you to a man, take my word for it."

He did not speak the British language very distinctly, but at last the barbarians caught the meaning of his words, and it discomposed them sadly.

It did not cause them at once to fly, as the Roman thought it would have done, but it made them combat under mortal terror, and whilst they fought they listened anxiously for any sound that might betoken the approach of horsemen.

The two Romans made some headway against their foes, for Claudius fought as only one maddened by desperation can fight, and his rescuer played the cool and collected game, and so well did he guard and parry that he proved himself to be next to invulnerable.

At last, however, though not before they were surrounded by a pile of British dead, his arm also grew weary of smiting, and he gazed upon the many foes still left unvanquished with almost despairing eyes.

There were still a good three dozen of them surrounding himself and Claudius, who showed no signs of giving way, although a full score of their companions had already bitten the dust : and now he saw by the gradually paling cheek of the Standard-Bearer, and his own rapidly lessening energies from loss of blood, that unless by some ruse he could overcome or disperse the barbarians the doom of both would be death.

He accordingly made his countenance light up with an expression of joy that he was far from feeling ; and exclaimed with energy—

" Hurrah ! hurrah ! they come, they come ! I hear the hoofstrokes of their galloping horses upon the grass ; in an instant they will be here, and then we will kill these barbarians to the last man, aye that will we !"

He spurred forward as he spoke, and slashed to the right and the left more energetically than ever with his keen double-edged sword.

But the Britons, many of whom understood his words, fancying in their terror that they really did hear the advancing gallop of a troop of horse, and knowing full well that if it chanced to be a cohort of the Roman cavalry their lives would not be worth a minute's purchase, broke and fled in all directions.

Then the Roman horseman who had dashed up so opportunely to the rescue of Claudius clutched the Standard-Bearer's bridle, and shouting—

" Bear up, my friend, an hour's gallop will refresh you ; we are not safe until we have put a good dozen miles between ourselves and these bloodthirsty barbarians," he urged his own brave steed to a wild gallop.

On and on they flew, still beside the left bank of the sparkling river, and to Claudius, bleeding as he was at every pore, it seemed as though forest, stream, and verdant glade glided under his black horse's feet like a landscape seen in a dream.

Occasionally his companion spoke to him words of encouragement and hope, but he saw him not, nor heard he a single word that was addressed to him ; more and more indistinct grew the fair landscape to his eyes, the hoofstrokes of the horses sounded like a composing lullaby, each moment growing fainter and fainter ; and at last conciousness forsook him, and he fell fainting to the ground.

CHAPTER XVII.
IN WHICH EACH WARRIOR NARRATES HIS ADVENTURES.

THE Standard-Bearer's companion immediately reined in the two horses, and urging to the ground fastened them to a sapling by their bridles. He then hurried to the assistance of Claudius, muttering as he did so—

" We have left the foe nine miles in our rear, at all events ; and on foot, even if they have sense enough to follow our trail, it will take them a good hour to come up with us. For that length of time, then, we are safe."

He knelt by the side of Claudius, even while he spoke, and examined his wounds. As he did so his face assumed a very long and anxious expression as he exclaimed—

" Why, the poor fellow can scarcely have an ounce of blood left in his body. I had no idea that he was wounded like this. By the gods, I must bandage them up speedily and stop the flow of blood, or he will be sped."

He lost no time, but set promptly about the work that had to be done. Tearing some of his own inner raiment and some of the Standard-Bearer's into strips, he plucked some dock leaves, thousands of which flourished near by, and placing them on the wounds strapped them tightly in their places, whereupon the blood immediately ceased to flow.

He then drew a flask from his pocket, and forcing the mouth through the lips of Claudius, he poured half its contents—red wine of Cyprus—down his throat.

The effect was soon perceptible ; Claudius gasped for breath, then his eyes opened, and he murmured—

" What, Eumolpus, is it you ?"

" Yes, my friend, it is Eumolpus, in all truth, turned up at the right moment, too, or else he is very much mistaken," was the reply.

Claudius closed his eyes again for a few moments, then opening them, he said—

" I am so glad that you are here, Eumolpus, both for my own sake and yours too ; for verily I had begun to fear that you were either dead or a captive."

" I have been the latter, and very nearly the former," was the reply ; " in fact, this morning, at sunrise, in company with two hundred and ninety-nine other horsemen, I was offered up as a burnt sacrifice to the great British god, Suetovid.

"But how did you escape such a terrible doom, Eumolpus?"

"Ah, thereby hangs a tale, Claudius; one which will take time to narrate."

"Well, I feel too weak to move for some minutes; so e'en tell it me now."

Thus urged, Eumolpus the centurion narrated all that had befallen him since Claudius had quitted him the preceding noon until that moment.

In return, the Standard-Bearer also told of his adventures with the moose and at the palace of King Seraptus, with his escape therefrom, the pursuit, the defence of the bridge, his encounter with Cassibelan and Stella, and how the former had presented him with the noble black charger which he now called his own.

When both these sturdy warriors had narrated their adventures Claudius felt strong enough to mount, and a few minutes later they were again on horseback, and riding through the forest once more, in the direction of Caer Lud.

CHAPTER XVIII.

CAUGHT SLUMBERING—RUNNING THE GAUNTLET.

By the time that Claudius Fulvius was sufficiently rested the perpendicular rays of the sun, piercing the green mountain foliage, announced that it was mid-day.

His wounds had long since ceased to bleed, and the soothing application of the dock leaves had eased him of much pain, so that he sat his horse without difficulty.

"We have still a start of our foes," he remarked at length to Eumolpus, the centurion; "and if there are not further ambuscades ahead of us, we have little to fear from enemies that are in our rear. I feel quite strong enough for another twenty miles' gallop before sunset."

"The King of Atrebatium, your old friend Cassibelan, and his three thousand horse and foot, cannot be far behind us," rejoined Eumolpus. "In your present weak and exhausted state, would it not be better to wait until they come up, and travel under their escort?"

"It might be safer, for these fierce Britons seem to have little regard for either flag of truce or safe conduct, but Cassibelan wishes me to arrive at the court of Cassivelaunus first, lest that monarch, if we travel in company, should suspect us of some secret understanding. Cassibelan's forces will, however, effectually cover our rear, so that our sole danger now lies in our front, and we can be scarcely more than forty miles from Lud Town."

"Let us on, then," replied Eumolpus; and urging their horses to a gallop, they swept once more adown the green forest vistas, and continued at a hard gallop for miles, until the bright sun glimmered redly in the west.

Then they drew rein to walk awhile their tired and foam-speckled horses, intending to camp out in the green woods, and within the labyrinthine mazes of the luxuriant undergrowth.

At last it grew so dark that it became useless to pursue the route farther, lest they should lose the track, and they, therefore, determined to put their project into execution.

They had not to ride far off the road to effect this, and presently they got into the midst of a little hazel grove, where they thought that they would be quite secure from any wandering tribes of Britons who might be overrunning the surrounding country.

They picquetted their horses to trees close by, and then throwing themselves down on the soft, green, dew-glistening grass, they were soon wrapt in deep and dreamless sleep.

How long this calm, peaceable slumber continued they knew not, but at length Claudius awoke to see the moonlight streaming down through a rift in the clouds high overhead upon a number of armed Britons, who surrounded them, two of whom had their short javelins poised above their prostrate bodies, ready to transfix them to the ground should they suddenly awake and attempt resistance.

It was a terrible position that in which they were placed, but Claudius Fulvius never lost his presence of mind for an instant; unperceived by the gigantic Briton who towered above his prostrate body he moved his hand through the thick grass, and plucked the mantle of the sleeping centurion, accompanying the act with a scarcely audible "Hist!"

Then Eumolpus also awoke, silently and imperceptibly, as his companion had done before him, and he also observed, with half-closed eyes, the terrible predicament in which they were placed.

They could hear the fierce Britons chuckling to each other over the success of their surprise, and by their voices they knew that there must be a good dozen of them. The heads of the javelins grasped by the two barbarians, who stood, one behind Claudius, one behind Eumolpus, often glittered just above their faces, and might at any instant be buried in their broad chests; and yet neither of these Romans' nerves quivered with either fear or anxiety.

Yet what could they do? how hope to escape the half-naked savages who had them at such a vantage? for in all probability, even before they could draw their swords or gain their feet they would be slain. They could not communicate to each other any plan of action, they dared not even look into each other's faces, for that glance might have been their last in life.

At last a brilliant idea struck Claudius; he stretched himself out as though in sleep, at the same time breathing heavily, and causing his right hand to wander as though instinctively to his sword-hilt, while he muttered as though dreaming of some past contest—with long pauses, and, now and then, a snore between each word—

"Gather—yourself—up—for a spring—Eumolpus! When I rattle my sword-hilt—in my sleep —that is the moment. A lightning movement— may yet throw—them off their guard."

He ceased, and a heavy snore from the centurion signified that he was understood.

Claudius continued to talk on incoherently for a few more seconds, and could hear the Britons laughing at the language they evidently did not understand.

At last, however, the Standard-Bearer raised his right arm on high as though battling with some imaginary foe, and brought his open palm down with a clatter on his brass scabbard.

'Twas the signal agreed on, and swift as a flash of lightning the bold Romans' swords leapt from their sheaths, and springing to their feet themselves with equal rapidity, both the British javelin-bearers were stricken down and slain before they could even make an attempt at resistance, while the ten surviving barbarians turned and fled.

CHAPTER XIX.

THE HUT IN THE WOOD.—A TERRIBLE DOOM.

"I HOPE our enemies have not destroyed or run away with our horses!" exclaimed Claudius, suddenly, after he and the centurion had congratulated each other on their escape.

"We must see, for that were a loss indeed," answered Eumolpus. "If they are gone, our danger in traversing so many miles of this infernal country, where every tree-trunk seems to harbour a foe, will be increased ten-fold. Come, Claudius, your words have made me anxious, let us at once proceed to the spot where we picquetted them."

It was not far distant, and when they reached it, to their joy both steeds were there, quietly cropping the short sweet grass, and looking greatly refreshed by their rest.

After an hour's vigorous riding tired nature could endure no more. They had neither of them enjoyed on an average more than an hour's rest of a night for a week past, and they now each of them felt that they required a short repose to prevent them from breaking down altogether on the ensuing day.

"What shall we do?" said Claudius. "Sleeping under the greenwood trees we have discovered, to our cost, on several occasions, to be highly dangerous. Yet where else can we repose?"

And they slept soundly till they were aroused by hundreds of armed men.

But this time they were safe. The Britons in whose midst they were proved to be Cassibelan's force, who had overtaken the Romans whilst they slept. They had resolved to halt there to give their horses breath.

After a rough repast and an hour's halt the Britons again resumed their march, Claudius and Eumolpus being now in their midst.

They were now only twenty-five miles distant from the court of Cassivelaunus and the great city of Caer Lud, and as it was still early morning Cassibelan hoped to reach it before nightfall.

The little army pressed on, therefore, at its utmost speed, and that was at a rate of at least four miles an hour, for the wild, agile Britons were capable of maintaining this pace, even in close rank, for a considerable time.

At noon they again halted once more, for the purposes of rest and refreshment, the former being partaken of lying down, for a sitting position was never a favourite one with the ancients, and the latter consisting of water from a neighbouring rivulet, with black bread and sun-dried meat.

Claudius sat by Stella's side, and being a little apart from the others, he was enabled to pour his tale of love into her ear, and to receive the blessed assurance that he was as dear to her as he had just told her she was to him.

They sat conversing for some time, but were at last interrupted by the approach of Cassibelan and Ala, who entered into conversation with the Standard-Bearer, and when they had departed, lo! Stella was gone too.

At that instant up came Eumolpus, saying—

"Hallo, Claudius, you are alone; the camp does not break up for another hour. Let us take a stroll to yonder temple, whose wall we see above the tree tops."

"With all my heart," answered Claudius. "The walk will refresh us both."

They sauntered away leisurely in the direction indicated by the centurian, but as they neared the pagan structure which Eumolpus had descried in the distance they heard cries issuing from out a thicket a little in front.

"On, on!" exclaimed Claudius. "It is the voice of some woman in distress, and much I fear me that the cries are those of Stella."

"Now Heaven forefend—it may not—it cannot be," responded Eumolpus, drawing his sword and listening intently for a recurrence of the sounds.

But Claudius stayed not to pause or listen; his flashing sword in his hand he sprang forward with the bounding step of a panther, and, followed by the centurion, burst through the thick undergrowth, and gained a tiny glade, whose grass was of the greenest, for the sun's rays penetrated not through the thick canopy of leaves that waved high overhead.

At one end of this green forest vista stood the temple, whose summit alone had, until now, been perceptible. It was formed of rough, unhewn, uncemented blocks of granite, and from within it rose a tumult of strange sounds.

These nor the building, however, attracted the attention of the two Romans; for there, in the very centre of the little open space, knelt a lithe, graceful female form, and over her stood a stern Druid with a bare knife in his hand.

One glance at the noble contours of that form, at the sweeping raiment white as snow, the tiny naked feet, the rounded arms bare from wrist to shoulder, and the circlets of gold that gleamed thereon, and the still brighter masses of golden hair that streamed adown her back in glossy waves to far below her taper waist, convinced

Claudius, though he saw not her face, that it was Stella, whose sweet young life the black-browed, bearded Druid was threatening.

"We want another victim," they heard the priest exclaim, wildly and fiercely, "and thou art evidently sent here by the gods for the especial purpose. We have one woman to fight the bear, another to combat the white bull, but we need a third to fling to the hungry wolves; therefore if thou wilt not accompany me uninjured thou shalt wounded to the temple of our goddess. Come, decide quickly!"

He brandished his knife aloft, and Claudius heard the low, sweet voice of Stella rejoin—

"Slay me now if thou wilt, for if I am to be torn to pieces by the fierce wolves, oh, let it be after death, not whilst I am still living."

"But the sacrifice will not then be sufficient. I will wound thee so as to prevent thee resisting me further, and then I will drag thee by thy hair into the temple, and throw thee wounded and bleeding amongst thy fierce foes. Trust me, child, thy sufferings will be brief, for they have not been fed for a week."

"But I am the Princess Stella, sister of King Cassibelan."

"It matters not. The more worthy will be the sacrifice and the more acceptable to the goddess."

Again the blue-bladed knife was raised aloft—again the beautiful Princess gasped, while her form vibrated with terror—

"Spare me! oh, spare me!"

"Not if thou wert thrice a princess. I will sheath my knife-blade in each of thy resisting arms, and then drag thee to the wolves, sister of a king thou thou art."

He raised his dagger to strike, but ere the weapon could descend his hand was cleft off at the wrist by the Standard-Bearer's unerring blade, whilst at the same moment Eumolpus sheathed his own weapon up to the hilt in the Druid's side, who instantly fell to the ground a corpse.

Stella sprang to her feet and threw herself in her lover's arms.

"Ever the barrier between me and death," she said, tenderly.

But at that moment piercing shrieks are heard from the interior of the temple, causing the very blood to curdle within the veins of the two Romans.

"Stella," said Claudius, "some terrible tragedy is being enacted within that grim old fane—some diabolical cruelties perpetrated. Run you back to camp, 'tis not a quarter of a mile distant, and no danger will threaten you now. Tell your brave brother to send a score of his warriors to our assistance, and, if possible, to come himself; our two swords shall meanwhile be drawn in the defence of beauty and innocence, and strike hard to stop the infernal rites."

"Oh, Claudius, consider the danger, and how dear you are to me," pleaded Stella.

"I should not be worthy of your love did I act otherwise than I am about to do. A Roman's sword is ever at the service of the weak and the defenceless."

"But promise me, Claudius, that you will not be too rash," she urged.

"I promise you that I will not expose my life to danger needlessly; that we will not interpose unless there is at least a chance of our interference being crowned with success," answered Claudius. "Now away, Stella, or 'twill be too late."

The Princess bestowed one lingering, fond embrace upon her lover, and darted away with the speed of a young panther adown the glade, thereafter dashing through the thickest of the undergrowth, unmindful of the scratches that her polished limbs received from the wild briars in her rapid transit.

"Off with the Druid's white robes," whispered Claudius, "and slit them in two down the middle, for they are ample enough for us both—aye! and to spare."

Eumolpus speedily obeyed his friend's commands, and a minute later the two Romans were draped from head to heel in the priest's vestments, out of which they had also fashioned cowls to draw over their gleaming helmets, and conceal, to a great measure, their beardless faces and short, crisply curling locks.

"Now, hey for the temple," cried Claudius, "and woe be to those who are maltreating innocent women or children therein, if our swords can but reach them."

Exciting no suspicion, clad in their Druid robes, Claudius and Eumolpus made their way into the interior of the grim Pagan temple.

They found it to be a vast roofless building, built of granite, with a great sacrificial altar here and there, and at present crowded with people.

In the centre was a circular arena, roughly palisaded round to a considerable height, and strewn with mingled sand and pebbles.

This arena was empty, but presently hundreds of voices cried, "She comes, She comes! 'tis the vestal virgin who hath volunteered to combat the fierce brown bear."

As they spoke, a young girl, who could scarcely have numbered eighteen summers, with a beautifully developed form, and long golden hair, entered the arena.

She was armed only with a short double-bladed knife, and her sole attire was a short garment which extended from the waist to half way down the thighs.

CHAPTER XX.

INSIDE THE TEMPLE—FIGHT BETWEEN A WOMAN AND A BEAR.

THE instrument the girl grasped was about two feet long and full three inches wide, gradually diminishing towards the point and the handle.

She bowed to the audience and stood in an imposing attitude; her stately and rounded figure drawn up to its full height, her shoulders well thrown back, her broad fair front expanded, her left hand resting gracefully on her hip, while her right, grasping the glittering blade, was raised proudly on high.

Her body fairly glistened with the oil that had been rubbed over it, in order to promote the elasticity of the limbs, and as she bounded into the arena the action of the muscles was perceptible with every movement, whilst the freedom of her gait and the few contortions which she practised preparatory to taking her final stand showed that she posessed uncommon activity, combined with no ordinary degree of strength.

The expression of her countenance was actually sublime when she gave the signal for the bear to be let loose; it was the very concentration of moral energy, the index of a high and settled resolution.

She raised her right arm thrice as a signal for her terrible antagonist to be admitted into the arena, and at the third elevation of the snowy and rounded limb the bars of a large cage at the opposite extremity of the circle, were instantly lifted from above, and a huge brown monster emerged from the dark den. Rearing itself upright on its haunches it slowly advanced in a perpendicular attitude towards its human foe, every hair seeming to stand erect upon its back as it indulged in angry though suppressed growls.

"Shall we interfere?" inquired Eumolpus of his friend in a whisper.

"We have no cause to; the girl is evidently a willing combatant. She attempts no more than many a patrician lady of Rome has done in the Colliseum," answered Claudius, with a shrug of the shoulders; "but she will assuredly be slain."

The girl and the bear were now within a dozen paces of each other.

Bruin halted and looked first at his opponent and then at the surrounding galleries, wherein Druids, priestesses, warriors, and peasantry, from the child of five to the grandsire of four-score, were seated to watch the sports.

The bear, however, did not appear at all easy in its present state of freedom, and was evidently confounded at the novelty of its position.

After a short pause of indecision, it turned suddenly round and waddled back to its cage, in the same ungraceful attitude in which it had advanced.

In vain the Druids' armed servitors, who stood above, beyond the reach of mischief, tried to force it out again—all their efforts were in vain.

As a last resource they dropped the bars and threw several lighted pieces of tarred wood in amongst its shaggy fur; the bars being then again raised and the beast urged forth by flashing fiery torches in his rear.

Feeling the blazing fragments of tarred wood at last burning his skin, the bear now trotted into the arena with terrible roars and yells; a flaring torch was thrown towards the girl combatant, who caught it deftly by the handle, nor shrank for an instant from the pain as a hundred fiery sparks fell upon her own naked and oil-glistening form; nay, she flourished it round her head, standing in a perfect cataract of fire, while the bear leaped, turned, and writhed, as if in a state of frantic excitement, and at length crouched in a corner, uttering piteous growls, and sometimes snarling as a cat does when alarmed.

Meanwhile its retreat had been cut off by securing the door of its cage.

At last the beautiful young girl fixed the eye of her grim enemy, and began to advance upon him with slow but firm and determined steps.

The bear roused itself and retreated, the fur on its back standing erect, its mouth wide open, and its red tongue lolling out, a terrible sight to behold.

It seemed not at all disposed, however, to commence hostilities, but its resolute foe, girl though she was, was not to be easily evaded.

Fixing her eyes intently upon the deadly creature, she advanced with the same measured step, the bear retreating as before, but still presenting his front to the foe, while this little red eyes glared fiercely upon her.

At last the maiden suddenly halted, and instead of advancing, began to move slowly backwards, as though to make the bear think she was afraid.

Then the beast again reared himself upright, and began to advance in turn, uttering low growls, and at last evidently meditating mischief.

The girl continued to retire, flaring brand in one hand, knife in the other, but as soon as she was at so great a distance that the fixed expression of her eyes was no longer distinguishable the ferocious and now unawed brute made a sudden bound forward, crouched, and sprang toward her with a low, sharp growl.

But the girl, fully prepared for this, leaped agilely on one side, and as the bear, disappointed of its hug, came heavily down on all-fours, she swept round behind its bulky form, described a curve with her short but sharp-bladed knife around its near hind leg, and effectually hamstrung her grim foe.

The sinews were completely severed, and the bear was effectually prevented from again uprearing himself into his usual favourite fighting attitude.

The wounded beast roared, but turning suddenly on his assailant, who had by this time retired several yards, advanced fiercely upon her, his wounded leg dangling uselessly, and dropping blood gouts on the the thirsty sands of the arena.

Excited now to a pitch of reckless rage, the bear rushed, with incredible speed for a beast of its bulk, on its three legs, towards his beautiful adversary, who stood with her red knife upraised, calmly awaiting the deadly encounter.

As soon as the savage creature was within reach, as soon as she could feel its hot fœtid breath on her bare chest, she drew her arm back with lightning rapidity, and, as the bear rose, with tottering and uncertain balance, on its still serviceable hinder leg, to embrace her in its grasp of death, she took a step foward till her white bosom pressed against the shaggy breast of her foe, and disregarding the heavy paw which thudded down on each of her shoulders, until the great strong claws were deeply embedded in her soft flesh, she gave one desperate underthrust and drove her knife into the bear's body, up to its very hilt

With a low groan the huge animal fell backwards on the sands of the arena, dragging the young girl-warrior with him, but the beast was dead, and she soon disengaged herself from its embrace. Rising to her feet, she coolly wiped her knife on the animal's hide, made a dignified bow to the spectators, and amid thundering acclamations from Druids and people alike, retired with firm step from the arena, though her face was as pale as death, her chest heaved wildly with the excitement and exertion she had just passed through, and from her erst beautiful but now lacerated shoulders streams of blood ran down her body, falling with a " drip ! drip !" on the ground as she walked.

CHAPTER XXI.

THROWN TO THE WOLVES.—TWO BLADES TO A HUNDRED.

THERE ensued a pause of a few minutes' duration and then another female, also young and beautiful, entered the arena, garbed, or rather ungarbed, like her predecessor, upon whom was turned loose a spirited white bull.

The animal charged down upon her like an avalanche ; she sprang on one side and lunged with her short copper sword at his heart ; but the blade glanced aside against a rib, and she fell forward on her face.

In an instant she was on her feet again ; but by this time the fierce bull had doubled round, and ere she could resume her guard he caught her body and tossed her high in the air, catching her again on his horns as she fell.

She was transfixed thereby, and a torrent of blood deluged the bull's curly face and formed a pool in the yellow sand. With a dying groan she fell to the earth, and the fierce brute had, in a minute, trampled her lovely form into a shapeless mass.

Then the beast was captured by noosed ropes being thrown over his horns, and led back to his den, while the mutilated corpse of his victim was dragged by iron hooks to the spoliarium, leaving a long track of blood behind it.

* * * * * *

Again there ensued a pause of a few minutes' duration, during which the Druids and priestesses seemed strangely discomposed ; but at length the audience began to shout, " The wolves, the wolves, where is their victim ?"

" My friends, we have no victim for the wolves," at length responded a Druid.

But the dissatisfaction of the populace then became apparent in a marked degree, and some hesitated not to shout that a victim must be found.

A volunteer was then called for, but none offered herself ; and as the victim was obliged to be a woman, the crowd at last began to demand that a priestess should be chosen by lot and cast in amongst the ravenous brutes.

Then the priestesses, fearful that one of their number might, by the very force of circumstances, be called upon to play the rôle of victim, raised the counter-demand that the girl who had battled so bravely with and defeated the bear, should again be brought into the arena, and thrown, unarmed, amongst the wolves.

This suggestion the Druids, the Eubates, and the bards echoed and supported for their own selfish interests, and the beautiful young girl, still clad only in her short coloured drawers, reaching from waist to hip, her shoulders scarred with the bear's claws, and her skin disfigured with lines of red blood, was a second time dragged forth, and hurled by strong hands into the arena.

Faint with the loss of blood, she staggered to her feet, but as she did so the bars of six iron cages were raised, and half a dozen lean, hungry wolves dashed out of them into the very centre of the circle.

The beautiful young girl was weaponless ; she knew that she was doomed to certain death, and she wrung her hands and shrieked aloud.

The audience applauded, the priestesses clapped their hands in glee, the Druids laughed grimly to each other, and passed the jest around.

The wolves opened wide their lank jaws, and from every point of the compass rushed, openmouthed, upon their victim, whose form quivered in mortal terror, and whose face blanched as the wolves came rushing on.

But ere one of the fierce beasts could lacerate her tender flesh with teeth or talons the two Romans, throwing their disguises to the winds, leapt, sword in hand into the arena, and stood between her and death.

For a minute or two, Druids, priestesses, and spectators were so struck with amazement and dismay, that they sat in open-mouthed astonishment gazing at the two chivalrous Romans who had so freely imperilled their lives to save one of their countrywomen, the lovely British girl, whom they had sentenced to death.

Then their bewildered and pent-up feelings found vent in a perfect roar of anger and indignation, which shook the old ivy-wreathed temple to its very foundations.

Meanwhile, Claudius and Eumolpus, shield and sword advanced, defied the fierce wolves to the combat, and right quickly was their rash challenge accepted.

With deep-toned barks and savage growls the half-starving beasts attacked them, without a moment's hesitation ; but not even the scaled rhinoceros could have presented a more impenetrable front to his foes than did the two Romans.

The wolves sprang at their human antagonists until their noses touched those of their reflected images in the bright steel shields that were opposed to them ; but at the same instant the sharp short-bladed Roman swords were thrust into their bodies with an under lunge, and they fell on the sand dead or disabled.

In less than three minutes the half-dozen wolves had been disposed of, and the two Romans, heedless that they were surrounded by a thousand foes, who had already risen as one man, crying aloud for their blood, turned to console and succour the brave British maiden.

Eumolpus supported her in his strong arms, for she was too weak from loss of blood to be able to stand, and spoke to her rough but kindly words of sympathy, swearing by Rome's gods that he would protect her with his life from Druids and priestesses alike.

A sweet smile stole over her beautiful but now pallid countenance. Doubtless the handsome, smooth-shaven Roman, in all his glittering panoply of scarlet, brass, and steel, looked to her like one of those demi-gods she had oft heard her island bards sing of.

Short time had she, however, wherein to conjecture who her valiant deliverers could be, for an arrow, shot by an unseen hand, quivered through one of her fair white arms, up to the very feathers at its head, eliciting a sharp cry of intense pain.

With a curse at his thoughtlessness Eumolpus covered her body with his shield on one side while Claudius performed the same kindly office on the other; and not a moment too soon were they, for a cloud of arrows and javelins darkened the air, falling upon the upraised shields of gleaming steel like hailstones mingled with thunderbolts.

"Leave me, oh! leave me to my fate, or you also will be slain!" exclaimed the British girl.

"We would not desire a nobler end than perishing in the defence of youth and beauty," answered Eumolpus.

But scarcely had he ceased speaking when the rain of arrows and javelins suddenly ceased, and the wild cries for blood and vengeance thundered forth by Druids and priestesses against the bold Romans who had dared so sacrilegiously to disturb the religious rites they had been celebrating, were turned into ejaculations of surprise and alarm, a mad stampede from the temple followed, and looking up Claudius and Eumolpus saw the towering form of Cassibelan and the graceful and undulating figure of the Princess Stella at the head of hundreds of wild warriors, bounding down over the successive tiers of rough wooden seats to their rescue.

A moment later they were surrounded by friends, and the Romans surrendered the form of the girl gladiator to the gentle hands of Stella, who rested the head of the beautiful sufferer on her own white breast, while she gently withdrew the arrow from her arm and poulticed and bandaged her wounds with some simple herbs that grew close by in the forest, and with fragments of her own raiment.

"It will never do to leave her here," remarked Cassibelan; "for directly we are gone the Druids or priestesses would return, seize upon her, and yet carry out their horrible sentence in some way or other. What say you, Stella? shall we take her with us?"

"I was about to propose it, my brother," answered Stella. "I have a spare palfrey which will bear her as easily as though she lay in a cradle, and I myself will tend her with the kindness and care of a sister. Come, my brother, let us be moving."

Eumolpus bestowed on the fair Princess a glance of deep gratitude, and he and Claudius then raised the wounded girl in their arms, and bore her out of the temple.

Here Claudius resigned his share of their fair burthen to a sturdy Briton, and fell back to say a few words to Stella, who was just issuing forth from the temple in the rear of all the others.

He had determined then and there to tell her of the deep love and affection that he entertained towards her, and to learn the worst at once, for how could he, a humble Roman standard-bearer, hope to win the hand of a haughty and high-born British princess?

And yet he did hope, even against hope, that Stella so loved him that she would be his in spite of the great gulf that at present separated them, seeming to form an impassable barrier in the future.

When he gained Stella's side she was still lingering just outside the temple; he advanced silently, and taking her hand in his said, "Stella, I have much to say to you, and yet it must not be said here, for we must closely follow up your brother's warriors lest the Druids and their followers return, cut us off from our friends, and slay us without mercy."

"Heavens! it is too late, for already are we so cut off," answered the Princess, pointing to two naked Britons, who, javelin in hand, were creeping up to them from behind the bushes.

Cassibelan's rear-guard was a good two hundred yards away, and these two painted warriors were evidently intent upon slaying the Roman soldier and the Princess where they stood.

They had reared their tattooed bodies, fierce vengeful faces, and muscular arms, whose hands poised aloft the deadly javelin, above the bushes by this time, ready to hurl their weapons at Claudius and Stella; but raising her from the ground with his left arm, the Roman Standard-Bearer, sword in hand, dashed at them. They essayed to bar his passage in vain; down went one with three inches of cold steel in his heart, and the other with his right arm lopped off at the shoulder.

A minute later Claudius had caught up the rear-guard of Cassibelan's little army, and then, and not till then, did he gently deposit the beauteous Stella on her feet.

The opportunity of coming to an explanation with her on the subject of his love was now, however, gone—gone, perhaps, never to return, for in another three hours they would be at the royal court of Caer Lud.

At length the cavalcade wheeled into a sort of oblong square, and there, right in front of them, stood the long, irregularly constructed palace of King Cassivelaunus.

It was only one storey in height, and was built entirely of wood on a foundation of stone.

Its roof seemed to be composed of porcelain, and not a window nor chimney was discernible.

In front of the building was a gigantic postern gate, and before it Prince Ala now wound his horn right merrily, awakening a hundred echoes around.

The gates quickly rolled open, and a momentary glance was caught of an inner court, but the aperture was quickly filled with savage, bearded, and tattooed warriors, who, upon recognising their youthful prince, uttered loud and clamorous cries of joy and satisfaction.

Then, in turn, there strode forth a chieftain

glittering in barbaric pomp.

His reception of Ala was equally affectionate, but with it there was an appearance of sorrow and anxiety that he could not help expressing, even though he was evidently endeavouring to conceal it from his prince.

But Ala saw it at a glance, and exclaimed—

"My father, is he well?"

"Yes, as well as may be; but the emissary of King Seraptus has so incensed him against thee that I fear he will greet thee right sternly and harshly, my prince," was the reply.

"Never fear, my good friend, I and my friends here will soon appease his wrath, and the head of this emissary of my uncle Seraptus shall be sent back to him in pickle. Now go and tell my father that Cassibelan of Atrèbatium, his sister—the Princess Stella, my unworthy self, and two brave Roman officers are at his gates, and request an audience," said Ala.

The courtier bowed and bore in the message, in a few minutes returning to invite the whole cavalcade into the interior of the royal fortress.

Thereupon Cassibelan, Stella, Claudius, Eumolpus, Prince Ala, and the wounded girl, followed by the five hundred horsemen of Atrèbatium, entered the gate, and while the latter drew up in order of battle in the inner court the former were ushered towards the presence chamber of the King.

CHAPTER XXII.

THE PRESENCE CHAMBER—A JUST SENTENCE.

KING CASSIVELAUNUS sat on his throne of state in the largest apartment of his wooden palace, nor did he condescend even to rise when Cassibelan of Atrèbatium, wearing also a crown of gold above his ruddy locks, approached his footstool.

Cassivelaunus, monarch of the largest city and the fairest country in Britain, was not going to abate one tittle of his dignity towards a lesser sovereign like Cassibelan.

The latter was, however, equally proud, and advancing to within three paces of Cassivelaunus's throne, he came to a halt, and folded his arms upon his broad chest.

Then Prince Ala sprang forward with all a boy's enthusiasm, exclaiming,—

"My father, have you no word of welcome for the King of Atrèbatium, in whose train I have ridden hither, and who has been my very good friend and protector."

"The King of Atrèbatium is truly welcome within these walls," answered Cassivelaunus, now rising from his seat and holding out the right hand of fellowship, which Cassibelan grasped; "but as for you, Prince Ala, how came you to need protection? Was it that you dreaded the retributive vengeance of your uncle Seraptus."

"Faith, my royal brother, your brave boy is not one to fear the vengeance of any man, but, nevertheless, had it not been for the devoted bravery of one of these noble Romans, that vengeance would have assuredly been wreaked upon him, and you would now have been childless," answered Cassibelan, gravely.

"Nor should I have blamed the avenger. What right had he to slay, without provocation, an honoured noble of his uncle's household?" said Cassivelaunus.

"I did not slay him," cried Prince Ala, stepping manfully to the front, and confronting his angry father with a calm and unruffled brow; "on the contrary, he it was who, by my uncle's commands, essayed to kill me in my sleep. This Roman officer heard them hatch their infernal plot, and hurried to warn me. When the rascally chamberlain entered my room, and raised his dagger above my body to bury it in my heart, this Roman caught the descending steel on his own trusty blade, and sliced the assassin's head from off his shoulders. We then fled, and Claudius held a bridge alone against a hundred foes, hazarding his life in order to secure my safety. Then we fell in with the train of this brave king, and journeyed hither."

King Cassivelaunus stood in mute astonishment at his son's words; then, recovering himself, he held out his arms, and Ala sprang to his embrace. Folding him in his strong nervous clasp, Cassivelaunus pressed him thrice fondly to his heart, and thrice kissed his broad fair brow; then putting him gently aside, he once more seized Cassibelan's hand, and this time wrung it warmly.

"The brave Roman, my father—remember the Roman," murmured Ala.

"Come hither, my friend," said Cassivelaunus, beckoning to Claudius.

Thereupon the Standard-Bearer strode calmly up to the foot of the throne and there halted.

The British King gazed at him admiringly as he murmured—

"And did you do all this for a stranger—nay more, for a foe? Then art thou noble indeed."

"The Roman soldier acknowledges no foes, save such as he meets under battle harness on the red field of carnage. The fight over, and sword and shield laid aside, he regards all men, even those with whom he has lately so fiercely contended, as friends and brothers," replied the Standard-Bearer, proudly, drawing himself up to his full height.

"But you saved my gallant boy's life at the imminent hazard of your own."

"I have done so thrice, and would do so thrice three hundred times again," said Claudius. "A soldier who for five long years has worked his hardest to destroy life may be occasionally allowed the privilege of protecting or saving it."

"And so this treacherous brother of mine really intended to murder my son?"

"Aye, sire, and thereafter to journey hither to represent that the Prince had come to his death by accident, and once here to destroy you in turn," answered Claudius Fulvius.

"To slay me!—me, King of Caer Lud, here in my own city of forty-five thousand inhabitants—here in my own castle, surrounded by my trusty warriors! Nay, that part of thy story thou must have dreamed," said King Cassivelaunus, starting.

"Nay, sire, that did I not, for I heard Seraptus and his chamberlain coolly discussing the manner of thy death, and at last it was fully decided that it should be by dropping aquetta into thy soup or drink," answered Claudius, the Standard-Bearer, calmly.

"Now I believe thee, Roman," exclaimed Cassivelaunus, with a start ; "and, by my fay ! since Seraptus comes hither to-morrow, a right warm reception will we give him, though first we will cut off the head of his envoy, lest he should obtain speech of his master, and warn him in time to put him on his guard. But thou, my friend, must quit the Roman service, and call me thy lord, and, in consideration of the services thou hast done me and mine, instead of a rude soldier thou shalt be the first man in my dominions."

The Standard-Bearer shook his head sadly but proudly, saying—

"I would not prove a traitor unto Cæsar and the soldiers by whose side I have fought and bled, not even for thy throne, sire. Better honour and a bed on a cold battlefield than dishonour and a couch of down on a bedstead of solid gold. No, King of Caer Lud, I wish for no reward save the comforting thought that I have done my duty to the gods as well as to my Emperor, and perchance gained in addition the affection of this young Prince, if he will give it me."

"Thou hast it, though knowest thou hast it, Claudius," cried Ala, springing to his side and grasping his hand. "Next to my father I love thee more than aught in the world beside."

The King checked not his son's enthusiasm, but smiled at it, then laying his hand on the shoulder of the Roman he looked straight into his eyes and then over his tall, commanding, martial form, exclaiming, as he at last withdrew his fixed regard—

"And so thou art a specimen of that wondrous soldiery who have conquered the whole of Europe, and one day may, perhaps, be the masters of the world. Well, now that I have seen a Roman I am not surprised at the invincibility of Rome's legions ; were all our island warriors as faithful to their leaders as thou art to thine we might yet be able to resist the foreign yoke ; but that, alas ! they will never be."

Cassibelan shook his head in sorrowful concurrence with this opinion, but Cassivelaunus broke the silence by crying to his guards—

"Bring hither Orca, the ambassador from our brother King Seraptus. We would have speech with him, and that speedily."

To hear was to obey. Half a dozen fierce warriors rushed out of the hall, and presently returned, leading in Orca, the perfidious messenger from the court of Mowern.

He strode with stately arrogance into the midst of the assembly, but his cheeks paled and his knees trembled beneath him when his eyes rested upon Prince Ala and the Standard-Bearer.

"Here is my son Ala. Now assert in his presence that wherewith he is charged, and in return he will proffer his accusation against thee and thy master," said Cassivelaunus.

"I prefer no charge against him. Oh ! great King, have mercy and spare me, for I only did my master's bidding," exclaimed the trembling ambassador, falling on his knees.

"And when will thy master arrive at our royal court ?' demanded Cassivelaunus.

"To-morrow, an hour after sunrise," was the reply of the ambassador.

"Then it is high time that thy tongue be silenced for ever, lest, when he comes, thou contrivest to have speech with him before ourselves. Swordsman, come forth."

As he spoke a tall, gaunt form stalked forth from behind the King's chair, holding in his hand a ponderous sword nearly as high as himself.

This great weapon he drew from its sheath, dashing the scabbard clattering to the ground. then, digging the point into the floor, he leaned upon the hilt awaiting the command of the King.

Nor had he long to wait, for, disregarding the prayers for mercy, fervently uttered by the doomed man, as he prostrated himself at his feet, Cassivelaunus gave the fatal signal, and Orca was dragged to his feet by twenty willing and rough hands.

CHAPTER XXIII.-

THE DRUID'S LEGEND—THE PALACE IN FLAMES.

THE ambassador of Seraptus glared wildly, hopelessly around him, but he was kept in an upright attitude, and the executioner, striding to within a couple of paces of him, raised his sword to strike.

He gave one quick glance at the King to see whether he showed any signs of relenting, but the brow of Cassivelaunus was still dark and stern as night.

Then the wide copper blade, swayed with both hands, hissed through the air, and the man's head was severed from his body.

"Take away that carrion," said Cassivelaunus, "and throw fresh rushes on the floor ; enough of these disagreeable scenes for the present. Let all be harmony and bliss until my brother comes on the morrow, when verily, although of my own flesh and blood, I will not spare him."

At this moment a wild clashing of barbarous music rang through the palace, and the doors at the lower end of the room being thrown open disclosed the tables in the adjoining apartment laid for the banquet.

Then King Cassivelaunus, rising from his throne, offered his hand with courtly grace to the Princess Stella, and followed by Cassibelan, Claudius, Eumolpus, and Ala, they swept into the banqueting hall, where the long tables were spread with a rude but plentiful repast, characteristic of the time and people.

Then many of the high officers of the household crowded in through an opposite doorway, and every seat soon had its occupant.

The musicians took their places in the gallery, the officiating Druid of the palace his chair of state next to the King, and the signal was given by Cassivelaunus for the banquet to be commenced.

Unto a late hour was that rough feast prolonged ; the horn goblets of milk, cumri, and metheglin were quaffed again and again, and the song and jest went merrily round.

Thus sped the greater portion of the evening, but at last the festivities grew languid, the most mercurial spirit began to tire, and the sunniest to diminish of its brightness.

Some then proceeded to the chambers allotted to them, and others, whom wine and wassail had rendered sluggish and drowsy, slumbered in their seats, while the numerous torches and flambeaux, which had hitherto blazed with unmitigated splendour, began now to shed a dim, quivering, uncertain light. The minstrels, seeing their services no longer required, had, every one, soon departed, and a deep and impressive silence shortly succeeded to the late uproarious mirth. Then it was that the boom of the midnight breeze, heralding the storm, which was expected every moment to burst, might have been distinctly heard wailing around the great rambling wooden palace, accompanied by the waves of the Thames dashing with angry violence towards the distant sea.

Bright and repeated exhalations had been observed for some time playing upon the hot and turbulent horizon, which oftentimes startled from their slumbers King Cassivelaunus, King Cassibelan, the chief Druid, Claudius, and Eumolpus, who had all of them been dozing in their chairs.

Presently the storm, which had long threatened, broke forth with unparalleled fury, accompanied in its onset by a wild and searing flash of lightning, which shivered one end of the wooden hall to fragments, and lighted up the scene with indescribable brilliancy, causing every object to dance and reel before their eyes, before they were again the next moment hidden in profound darkness.

But, almost before the spectators of this terrible sight had recovered their equanimity and composure, loud cries rang through the fortress of "Fire! fire! the palace is in flames!"

CHAPTER XXIV.

BURNING LONDON.—THE FIGHT IN THE STREETS.—ESCAPE.

IN a moment all was dire confusion and dismay; every one sprang to his feet, and every one ran hither and thither in wild despair, not knowing what he was about.

The flames, by this time, had rendered everything as light as day, for the palace, being of wood, burnt freely, and the city, constructed as it was of the same inflammable material, threatened to follow its example, in which case the destruction of life would be something terrible.

Somewhat stupified by the deep potations of cumri and metheglin, of which they had found themselves bound in courtesy to partake at the banquet, it was a good five minutes before either Claudius or Eumolpus could fully realise their position, but when they did do so, the first thought of the Standard-Bearer was of Stella—of Eumolpus, the wounded British girl whom they had saved from the wolves.

"I know where the apartments of the women are situated," said the centurion, hurriedly;

"follow me, Claudius. To the rescue—to the rescue! we will save or die with them."

Right willing was the gallant Standard-Bearer to assist his friend to the utmost, for he had quite as precious a stake depending on the issue.

They rushed from the deserted banquet-hall, therefore, but were met in the corridor without, by Prince Ala, who exclaimed, hastily—

"Take care of yourselves, make your way into the streets and fly from the fated city. They whom you seek, my friends, are already in places of safety, and I stay only to save some of the treasure."

"But we will stay and help you, Ala," said the Standard-Bearer, laying a hand on his shoulder.

"No, no! I tell you, a hundred times, no! your presence here might be productive of evil to all of us; besides, why should you risk your lives needlessly, for at any moment the palace may fall in upon us? No, go; if not for your own sakes, for the sakes of the beauteous women whom ye love."

Thus urged, Claudius and Eumolpus turned fly, and soon escaped from the burning palace into the streets, which they traversed in wild haste, seeking to gain the river.

The flames had already spread from the palace to the surrounding buildings, and it was perceptible to the keen sight of the two Romans that the whole city was doomed to destruction.

So, too, evidently thought most of its inhabitants, and despair seemed to be universal; the streets resounded with piercing cries and lamentations; affrighted citizens ran to and fro, not knowing whither they went or what they sought. Here and there, too, they would meet pale-faced crowds, speaking together in low and subdued tones, and putting questions to each other with a manner which betrayed the most agonising feelings of fear, anxiety, and suspense.

They could also hear, amidst the deeper and graver tones of sorrowing men, the loud shrieks and cries of distracted women; here clinging to the knees of their husbands, lovers, and brothers, calling upon them for protection from violence; there pressing their unconscious babes to their bosoms, and supplicating Heaven to shield them from the impending and terrible danger.

As the two Romans fled down street after street the fire seemed to travel as fast as they; and the terror and alarm which had so suddenly pervaded the city soon increased tenfold.

There was a wild running to and fro of the citizens in distracted and futile attempts to carry off their valuables, and to find places of security for the helpless, but they only impeded each other's actions, and while they delayed the destroyer swept swiftly towards them.

Suddenly other sounds than those of distress and panic filled the air. It was the fierce cry for vengeance, the wild clamour of "Blood for blood! Death to the Romans!"

"It is they who have set fire to the city! Kill them! kill them! Hack them to pieces!" cried a crowd of half-naked British warriors, rushing, with weapons uplifted, upon the two Romans.

But Claudius and Eumolpus drew their broad

gleaming swords, and the former, by one down-right blow, clove a stalwart Briton's head in two, while the powerful Eumolpus drove his sword deep into another's brawny breast; and then, charging through the Briton's close array, they hurled them to right and left, and ran at their utmost speed down the street.

But their glittering mail and brilliant accoutrements shone so clearly in the red light of the conflagration, that the infuriated Britons had no difficulty in following on their track, and the crowd of pursuers swelled larger and larger, until at last more than a hundred savage warriors were thundering at their heels. Nevertheless, on and on they went, but were at last brought to a halt by another body of men, who wheeled round the corner of a street in front and cut off their retreat.

They were now hemmed in, and escape seemed impossible. So they stood back to back, their shields well advanced, determined with their swords to sell their lives as dearly as possible.

On came the foe, hooting, halloing, and uttering terrible anathemas, for they really believed that the two Romans had come to their city in the character of friends, and then had perfidiously set fire to it. They were, therefore, maddened to an intense pitch of rage, and quite ready to hack the two supposed incendiaries to pieces, could they but master and overcome them.

But the countenances of both the Standard-Bearer and the centurion were calm and un-ruffled as if no danger menaced them; and the wild barbarians were sensibly awed by a facial composure which they could not comprehend under the circumstances. They rushed upon them, however, from every point of the compass, and for a few minutes the ringing of swords, battle-axes, and javelins on helmets and shields of proof drowned even the roar of the conflagration, the falling of beams and rafters, and the wild shrieks and cries of panic-stricken women and frightened children.

Quickly the two Romans had to parry, cut, and thrust, and presently the heavy-nailed sandals that Claudius wore, affording but a treacherous foothold on the ground, already slippery with blood, caused him to slip, and he fell with a heavy back-fall to the ground.

"Habet!" exclaimed Eumolpus, striding over his prostrate comrade while he spoke, finding himself, in the act, engaged with a score of tattooed warriors, who, with loud and exulting cries, pressed yet more closely around them like a swarm of bees.

Claudius, however, covered his body skilfully under his shield, and defended himself still bravely with his sword, dealing more than one fatal thrust at such of his assailants as were rash enough to believe him vanquished because he was down; vain, vain delusion!

Yet still the slaughter of the two Romans was only a matter of time; already they bled from many wounds; then Eumolpus lost his helmet, and had enough to do from that moment in guarding his own head, without bestowing further

thought on Claudius, who managing to reel to his feet, was the next instant again stricken down by an athletic Briton, who would have dashed out his brains with his great club then and there, had not a sudden diversion been effected in the Romans' favour by half a dozen mounted horsemen, who dealt blows unsparingly right and left, and forced their way into the very centre of the scene of strife, interposing between the conquerors and the conquered.

"Rise, brave Romans we are here to save you," said the sweet clear voice of Ala, who rode at their head. "Claudius, mount before me. Eumolpus, get thee up behind my henchman, Staffa. Now, fellow Britons, hold off, I tell you; for these Romans are real men, and I will answer for their integrity with my life. Nay, you must take my word or my sword. Stand back there!"

As he spoke, partly by threats, partly by cajolement, Ala, with prancing charger, waving sword, yet frank and open smile, held the blood-thirsty citizens in check until Claudius and Eumolpus were both mounted, when, in obedience to his muttered command, the half-dozen horsemen urged their chargers to a gallop, and, breaking through the mob, descended the street at full speed.

On, on, with the flames leaping and the smoke curling around them, while huge timbers fell crashing down on every side of them, throwing up showers of sparkling embers as they fell, the very stonework of the foundations glowing and riven with heat, through all this they rode, with loud cries and shouts of agony and despair ringing in their ears, while occasionally men, women, and children would leap down from windows and blazing roofs, only to be dashed to pieces on the hard road or trampled under their horses' feet.

At last the galloping horsemen emerged from the blazing city, and in a moment a dark wide gulf appeared to open before them, and the roar of water burst upon their ears.

Then they caught a dim and indistinct glance of a wide foam-flecked river, stretching right before them, dark and turbid as the fabled Styx; and, almost ere the two Romans felt assured of the fact, they became aware that the horses upon which they were mounted were breasting its tide, and striking out boldly for the opposite, though invisible shore.

The double weight was, however, too much for the two double-laden steeds; and they had soon sank neck deep into the water, but upon their two British riders dismounting and swimming by their side, they rose again, and the southern bank of the river was at last gained, though not until men and steeds were exhausted.

All here was dark and still as death, great trees waved their boughs mournfully on high, and the wind wailed dismally amongst the distant oak forests, but not a token of a human habitation was visible, and only one solitary light was anywhere to be seen.

The light of the burning city did not penetrate so far, though it tinged much of the river with a ruddy light, reddening the whole of the northern heavens with its glow.

At last the fire was reached, and a group of people

were descried sitting around it. After the horse-men had dismounted and approached the cheerful blaze, these were discovered to be King Cassive-launus, King Cassibelan, the Princess Stella, and the wounded British girl.

The meeting between Cassivelaunus, Cassibelan, and Stella, on the one side, and Claudius, Eumol-pus, and Ala, on the other, was a very cordial one.

Cassivelaunus apologised for not considering the safety of the two Romans before his own, but ex-plained that his first thought was of the ladies of his household, and, after securing their escape, he had returned to the banquet-hall, but only to find it empty.

Claudius and Eumolpus had then to narrate their adventures in the burning city, the sequel of which was given with becoming modesty by the boy-prince who had saved them.

"And now," said Cassivelaunus, "though we have no longer a court, noble Romans, in which to receive you, you may enter fully into those matters which, on the part of your Emperor, you have hastened here through a thousand perils to lay before us. What would Cæsar have Cassive-launus do?"

"My presence may, perhaps, be undesirable during the controversy," said King Cassibelan, springing to his feet; "if so, noble Cassivelaunus, I will retire awhile from your camp-fire."

"Nay, I have no secrets from a brother-monarch, whose interests should be the same as my own," replied the King of Caer Lud; "there-fore, speak freely, Roman, and boldly perform thy duty to thy master, Cæsar."

CHAPTER XXV.

IN WHICH CÆSAR'S OVERTURES ARE REJECTED.

THUS adjured, Claudius unfolded to the lordly-looking British King the Emperor's proposals that he should unite with the Romans in their attempt to subjugate the whole of Briton, offer-ing the tempting bait of the viceroyship of the island, in the place of his own petty sovereignty, when that result was achieved, and free England turned into a Roman province.

Claudius argued boldly, ably, and attempted, as in duty bound, to make black appear white, as thoroughly as a nisi-prius lawyer could do at the the present day, when pleading on the wrong side.

Cassivelaunus listened with the utmost patience, until he had concluded, with such patience and suavity, indeed, that the Standard-Bearer began to feel confident that he should succeed in his mission, and not until nearly five minutes after he had concluded was he undeceived.

Then Cassivelaunus, turning to Cassibelan, said quietly—

"Brother, these warriors journeyed hither in thy train. Have they made similar proposals unto thee on behalf of their Emperor, and did you give them heed?"

"I spurned them with the scorn and contempt they merited, and had it not been for the great respect, mingled with deep affection, that I felt for the ambassadors, who have thrice saved me and mine from death, I should have hung them as fitting acorns from the branch of one of our largest forest trees," replied the fiery Cassibelan, with flushed cheeks and frowning brow.

"And did you not tell them, my brother, that an appeal to me would be equally fruitless?"

"I did, Cassivelaunus, but I could not dissuade them from performing the duty which they owed to their master, and which they were determined to fulfil at whatever peril to themselves; so I brought them hither in my train—I, a British King, and one, too, who would die in defence of his native land, knowing, oh, Cassivelaunus, that you yourself were equally loyal to Britain, and that in doing this deed I did not endanger Britain's cause or liberty. I thought also," he continued, in milder tones, "that you would like to see, and personally to thank, the man who had saved the life of your only son."

"And, by Mars, you thought rightly, Cassi-belan," rejoined Cassivelaunus, grasping the hand of Claudius. "Noble Roman, I scorn the pro-posals of your Emperor, even as my brother-monarch does. I will hold no terms with Cæsar, save with my sword point at his throat; but this has nothing to do with the personal friendship I feel for thee. Remain at my court, and thou shalt be the first one in my dominions, even as I before promised thee. Nay, reflect before you return me an answer, for by doing so you will escape the de-struction and annihilation which is about to befall thine army of invasion."

"Destruction!—annihilation!—what mean you, sire?" stammered Claudius, aghast.

"Why, that even while I speak thousands and tens of thousands of our hardy island warriors, under cover of our dark woods, are creeping up stealthily towards Cæsar's camp by the sea, and surrounding it. They already outnumber the Roman forces by ten to one, and by to-morrow's eve that army will be doubled, when King Cassi-belan and myself join it with all our followers. Well, Cæsar's fleet is not ready to put to sea, and when our army, in one vast crescent, charges down upon his cohorts, they will be driven into the waves and the quicksands, and not a Roman will survive to tell the tale."

"Heavens, this is terrible! We must away to share their fate," cried Eumolpus.

"Yes,—yes, gracious monarch, give us leave to depart at once?" echoed Claudius.

"But you will not arrive in time to save them," said Cassivelaunus, in blank astonishment.

"But we may in time to die with them," answered Claudius and Eumolpus in a breath.

"Romans, you are mad! If you cannot aid your friends, what is the use of your merely rush-ing away to perish with them?" grunted Cassive-launus, "particularly you, oh, Claudius, whom, as a reward for saving my son's life, I have pro-mised to make the first man in my kingdom; aye, and your friend here, with the unpronounceable name, shall be the second, if you will but stay."

"And I will regard you as a brother, Claudius," said Prince Ala, striding up and taking the standard-Bearer's right hand. "Think again over my father's proposition, and stay with us, I beseech you."

Then the beautiful Stella in turn glided up to the Standard-Bearer's side, and taking his left hand, whispered in his ear—

"Oh! Claudius, stay in Britain, amongst your friends. If you return to the doomed Roman camp, I shall never see you more. Oh! stay amongst us, and I will be your bride."

Claudius felt his heart rise in his throat, as he felt himself bound by honour to refuse even this last appeal from one he loved even more than life.

On the one side were power, position, ease, comfort, the friendship of kings and princes, and a union with a lovely girl whom he fondly loved; on the other, dangers, perils, and hardships to be endured in striving to regain the Roman camp, and a terrible death amongst thousands of his countrymen, even if he did reach it.

Yet was the brave Standard-Bearer never for an instant indecisive as to the course which he should adopt. He pressed Ala's hand, bent a long lingering glance of affection upon the beautiful Princess, and then drawing his sword, raised it and his eyes on high, whilst, as one inspired, he raised his voice in a full fierce cry, that seemed to combine the shout of triumph with the wail of suffering, and to bid a long and hopeless farewell to earth and all its loved remembrances, even in the very recklessness and defiance of its despair.

"*Ave Cæsar! Morituri te salutant!*" (Hail, Cæsar! those who are to die salute you!)

Often had he heard the gladiators raise this shout in the great amphitheatre at Rome, as they halted with military precision to range themselves in line under the Emperor's throne, ere they engaged in those stern and terrible encounters which, to every second man, meant death; and with a gladiator's reckless daring was he now imbued, when love, friendship, and every fond emotion of the heart called him one way, and the inexorable voice of duty alone beckoned him the other.

"*Ave Cæsar! Morituri te salutant!*" echoed Eumolpus, swayed by the same emotions.

The voice of his companion restored Claudius to perfect calmness. He raised Stella's hand to his lips and kissed it respectfully, then motioned her to resume her seat beside her brother.

He pressed Ala's hand, and murmured—

"No, no, dear boy, it cannot be," and then said, quietly—"King Cassivelaunus, on behalf of myself and my friend, I thank you for you kindly offers, but neither I nor he can accept them; duty is a soldier's polar star, and duty compels us to return to the Roman camp, and to share the perils, and if need be, the doom of our fellows. Our mission here is accomplished, you decline the proposition made unto you by our emperor. We beg, therefore, that you will permit us to return to Cæsar's camp, under your safe conduct, and that with all speed."

"You shall do so," said Cassivelaunus, with emphasis, "and without a single restriction being laid upon you as to what you shall or shall not reveal if you reach your friends before our meditated attack. Put Cæsar even on his guard if you will, for it will not avert the fate to which he and his army are doomed, and I, for one, would sooner battle with the lion when he is awake and prepared to meet me with fangs and claws ready sharpened, than steal upon the noble animal and stab him treacherously to the heart while he sleeps. Do I echo your sentiments, Cassibelan of Atrebatium?"

"To the letter, oh, Cassivelaunus," replied that monarch, with enthusiasm.

"Then you shall depart directly day dreaks in the east," said the King of Caer Lud, again turning towards Claudius and Eumolpus, "on two of my fleetest steeds, under my safe conduct, and with a trusty guide to show you the way. So now take my advice, and try to snatch a little sleep, so that you may the better be enabled to bear the toil and fatigue of the morrow."

This advice was too sound to be neglected, and so Eumolpus stretched himself at once on the ground before the camp fire, and Claudius, after a few words with Stella, in which she in vain endeavoured to break his resolution, followed his comrade's example, and, strange as it may seem, not five minutes had elapsed before they were both of them buried in a profound slumber.

CHAPTER XXVI.

CLAUDIUS DREAMS A DREAM OF STRANGE IMPORT.

A STRANGE vision appalled Claudius that night. He dreamed that he had risen from before the camp-fire and had pursued the winding of the forest for nearly an hour with unabated speed; at length he had halted, finding himself still involved amidst its labyrinths.

He glanced around him, eager to discover some outlet, but he sought in vain. He cast his eyes above, yet he saw nothing but the closely twisted branches of the trees, and below him the heathy sward, illumined still by the broad flare of conflagration which wavered fiercely over the landscape, making the moonlight pale and ghastly. Broader and broader yet seemed to grow the red blaze of the burning city, while the cries, groans, and shouts of the distant populace were plainly audible.

The birds and beasts of the grim forest were all awake and astir, the distant howl of the wolves could be distinctly heard, with the growl of the brown bear, the conch-like trumpetings of the moose, while troops of half-wild horses, with coal-bright eyes, streaming tails, and tossing manes, stood revealed in the portentous blaze, which the red Thames reflected to the umbered skies, and then snorting, wheeling, and careering up and down, seemed as though they would stem the fire-lit stream, to join in the scene of commotion. The raven's huge black wings might be seen in the glare, sailing slowly along, the awakened hawk stretched his long pinions as his bright eye looked forth from his brown oak, while the great owl was hushed, and the cruel otter, trembling in his bulrush haunt, deemed that the morning's hunt was about to be resumed.

He gazed upon the heathy sward, which the ruddy light, streaming through an opening here and there, beautifully chequered. At his feet he beheld a crystal spring bubbling and flashing through the tall grass.

He bent his knee, and bathed his hands and face therein, but the cooling fluid refused to refresh him.

Then he thought that the forest was suddenly wrapped in profound gloom, so that he lost his way, and the only course left open to him was to abide where he was until daybreak.

As this, however, was a measure which he felt by no means disposed to adopt, he still continued to stumble on in the darkness, hoping in his dream that he might somehow be able to regain the camp fire, beside which he had laid himself down to sleep so short a time previously.

At last the breeze seemed to subside, the waving of the trees became inaudible, and even the murmur from the distant city dwindled into a dreamy indistinctness, and a silence, terrific and profound, presently involved the scene.

But anon the scenery seemed again to brighten up before him, and a bluish trembling lustre gradually expanded, imparting a preternatural tinge to the landscape.

Then footsteps sounded on his ear, and anon someone seemed to cross the path in front of him, and he felt himself shuddering violently, while a terror which he could by no means withstand, gradually crept over him; his every nerve seemed paralysed, he felt himself unable to speak or move, and he leant passive against the trunk of a gigantic oak tree.

Presently two shadowy forms were discerned flitting dream-like to and fro before him. Anon they became more defined, and eventually took the appearance of armed figures striving hotly against each other.

One of the combatants was a Roman, with crested helm, gleaming mail, scarlet raiment, and short double-bladed sword; the other was a naked tatooed Briton, with a cap of iron, shield of tough, brass-bossed bull's hide, and a gleaming axe, which he whirled madly around his head, pressing his antagonist with blow on blow with great rapidity.

The weapons of the spectral combatants struck forth sparks of fire with every blow, though no sound whatever of the strife was audible. Thus they contended for the space of several minutes when, all at once, the Roman warrior stumbled over a piece of rock, which the tall grass concealed, and his opponent, instantly following up the advantage, clove his helm in twain.

The shivered casque rolled on the ground, the lustre became more brilliant and gleamed vividly on the visage of the prostrate warrior, and one glance showed the amazed Standard-Bearer a perfect resemblance of his own face, armour, and trappings.

A glittering cortége of British warriors and maidens then appeared to advance, and one of the latter was received exultingly into the arms of his savage conqueror

In a moment the lustre fled, and profound darkness again took possession of the scene.

At last, with a start, Claudius awoke from his dream-tortured slumber. He rubbed his eyes but it was some time before he could bring himself to believe that fancy had been playing her pranks upon him. It could not have been real; it must have been some unaccountable delusion, he argued with himself, for there stood the trees, the copse, and the brushwood, waving their autumnal foliage in the grey light of early dawn; there too, were the streams he had before witnessed twinkling merrily by and catching and reflecting the gleams that began to streak the eastern heavens.

No trace whatever of the phantom combat was visible, and though blood had seemed to flow profusely from the wounds of the combatants, not a stain was there seen on the velvet sward.

Claudius, therefore, succeeded at last in convincing himself that the scene he had lately witnessed was in all reality a dream, and that his late mysterious antagonist and conquerer was no other than a being which his fancy had conjured up in his sleep-benumbed brain.

He lay some time awake, scarcely liking to disturb the slumber of the two Kings, although he felt that every moment's delay might be of the utmost import to the Roman cause.

Whilst he lay thus the tramping of many hoofs resounded in the distance, and, turning his head, he descried a cavalcade of some dozen mounted men riding straight towards them, adown one of the green forest vistas, that was illumined now by the first rays of the morning sun.

As they drew nearer Claudius recognised in the foremost horseman the form and features of King Seraptus of Mowern, and he therefore thought it was high time to awake his companions.

Men were light sleepers in those days, when to slumber with both eyes and ears closed was, perhaps, to slumber for ever, and in an instant the two kings, with Prince Ala, Stella, and Eumolpus, the centurion, were awake, and acquainted with who was approaching them.

"The traitor!" hissed the boy-Prince; "he thinks I have not escaped the toils he set for me, and now he comes to thy court, my father, to condole with thee on my untimely fate, and in turn to brush thee from his path, by dropping his accursed aquetta into thy soup. Oh, let me at him, sword in hand!"

"Not yet, my boy," said Cassivelaunus calmly. "He has doubtless not seen thee, so get behind this great oak, and thou bold Roman also; I fain would hear what he has to say, and at the proper moment I will call ye both forth to confute him; be still only a little while."

Both Ala and Claudius promptly complied with the King's request, and they had scarcely hidden themselves when the King of Mowern, surrounded by his courtiers, was close by.

Claudius, looking from behind the tree, noticed the face of Seraptus was very pale, and that there was a nervous twitching about the corners of his mouth, that, with all his pains, he could not conceal. He was surrounded by just a dozen fol wers, and amongst them Claudius recognised e faces of many of the monarch's most trusted visers, who had sat close around him at the nquet table in the castle. They were all well ounted, and armed to the teeth.

Seraptus had long ago perceived the camp fire nd the group around it; but not until he came ose by did he recognise the fact that two kings, lovely princess, and a gorgeously-arrayed Roman ldier formed the incongruous assembly who had urted the ruddy blaze.

"Cassivelaunus, my brother, is it thee?" he ied, dismounting from his grey steed, and ad-ancing with outstretched hand towards the ing of Caer Lud; "why, what brings thee, and such company too, to prefer the damp grass r a bed, and the vault of Heaven for a roof, stead of a couch of skins, and the oak rafters thy palace for a covering?"

"My palace is no more, my city is no more, and any of my people are in the same evil strait," nswered Cassivelaunus, pointing across the river wards the still burning city.

"Ah, I see you have had a fire! Well, what destroyed can easily be built up again, for ou have wood enough and to spare for the pur-ose; but alas! some losses cannot be repaired, nd I am unhappily the bearer of tidings to which he burning of thy city will be but as a trifle ght as air," was the reply of Seraptus.

"What is the nature of thy evil tidings? erily, one mishap ever follows another."

"Thy son—thy brave boy, Ala—is dead; I come bear thee the sorrowful news, my brother."

"Ah! that, indeed, is evil tidings; but tell he how he met his fate, Seraptus—tell me how he ied."

The King of Mowern started, and was con-iderably disconcerted at the calm manner in hich Cassivelaunus received the intelligence of he loss of his only child, but he quickly recovered is composure, and replied in a firm voice, whose very tone was marked with deep feeling—

"You heard from my first messenger how the passionate and headstrong boy, for a fancied in-ult, slew my chamberlain in cold blood. I hought fit, by virtue of the authority you gave e, to punish him for this offence in a way which suppose he though too severe. Anyhow, the ext day he fled from the castle. I sent after im a chosen band of dependants, to discover him nd bring him back. All in vain, however, was heir search, for after two days' zealous pursuit hey at last came across his skeleton lying in ront of the cave of a monstrous brown bear."

"How knew they that it was the skeleton of my son?" asked Cassivelaunus.

Again Seraptus was disturbed by the composed manner in which his brother asked the question, but he again answered, while the tears rose to his eyes,

"Only by fragments of his dress that lay around; by no other sign could he be recognised, for every particle of his flesh was consumed, and many of his bones had been broken by the fierce brute."

"You think, then, from these facts, that he was too dead to be restored to life!" said Cassi-velaunus.

The King of Mowern stared at the speaker in amazement; he thought that his brother must be mad.

"Too dead to be restored to life when all his flesh had been eaten by a bear, and nearly all his bones broken and crunched by the same cruel animal—why, yes, I do!" he replied, confusedly.

"He was not then, for behold him here. Ala, step forth," said Cassivelaunus, in a voice of thunder, and the young Prince, coming forth from behind the tree, faced his treacherous uncle.

The latter turned pale as death, and his knees smote each other; he could not speak a word.

"You seem astonished to see Ala so safe and well after his interview with bruin," said Cassi-velaunus.

Still Seraptus was silent, and Cassivelaunus, laying a grasp of iron upon his arm, said, sternly, "Brother, your tale is false. I accuse you of attempting my son's life."

"I, in turn, accuse him of murdering my chamberlain, and I have witnesses here who will support my asseverations," replied Seraptus, though again his knees smote together with terror.

"I, too, have witnesses who will prove that your chamberlain met his death even while stand-ing over the couch of my son, with his knife raised to take his life. Claudius Fulvius, stand forward and confute this man," said Cassivelaunus, sternly.

Then, in turn, the Standard-Bearer stepped out from behind the oak tree and confronted the King of Mowern, saying, "With my sword I took your chamberlain's life in defence of this boy Prince, and with that same sword I kept two hundred of your followers at bay for a quarter of an hour, and hurled a good half-dozen of them backwards adown an abyss, where their bones at this moment lie without sepulture. I also accuse you, King Seraptus, of coming hither with the avowed pur-pose of poisoning your elder brother, King Cassi-velaunus, and so joining his possessions on to your own, for I heard you avow your intention to do so."

King Seraptus saw clearly by this time that the game was up, and he essayed to shake off the tenacious clutch of his elder brother and to draw his sword upon him.

Vain the attempt; the grasp of Cassivelaunus was like that of a vice, and Seraptus saw that his other hand was stealing round his belt to where his dagger hung.

Then raising his voice, while the dark flush of passion overcame on his cheeks their previous pallor of fear, he cried to his followers as a last resource—

"Draw swords and axes! dash in and cut down these five fools who stand between us and wealth, honours, and estates! Here are two kings to slay instead of one; two accursed Romans also, and a beautiful princess to win, who shall be the play-thing of you all after the men are slain. Rescue me, rescue me! we are two to one; draw and strike in !"

Down came the mounted horsemen of Mowern like a herd of ravenous wolves upon their quarry, whirling above their heads swords, axes, and spiked war-clubs; but Claudius and Eumolpus threw themselves to the front, with their thirsty swords unsheathed, and their broad bright shields advanced, and the foe, though twelve to two, drew rein, and hesitated to advance.

Meanwhile, Cassivelaunus had drawn his dagger and raised it above his head to drive it into his false brother's breast, but at the last moment his heart relented. Seizing the opportunity, Seraptus succeeded in tripping him up, and they both came to the ground together.

Seraptus, however, was uppermost, and succeeding in drawing his own weapons, he with less feeling for his brother than that brother had entertained for him, raised the blue blade in the air, and with a hiss it descended towards its victim's body.

Rapid as was its descent another blade flashed through the air, however, still swifter; it was the sword of Prince Ala, which severed the dagger-hand of King Seraptus at the wrist, who gave a yell of mingled rage and agony, as hand and dagger fell on the green sward together.

The wounded King rose to his feet, and at the same instant his followers charged down upon the two Romans, whose terrible aspect alone had, until now, kept them at bay.

What, after all, could two foot soldiers do against a dozen horsemen? Down went one steed before the straight lunge of Claudius, and another before that of Eumolpus; then the surviving ten rushed down upon Cassivelaunus, Cassibelan, and Ala. But in a twinkling Claudius and Eumolpus had put an end to the existence of the two Britons who had been brought to the ground by the falling of their horses, and turned round to assist their hardly pressed friends.

Attacking the foe in the rear, they hamstrung their horses, while they protected themselves from descending swords, axes, and clubs with their upraised shields. They were a most effectual assistance in this way, for presently the whole party were dismounted, and many a tattooed warrior of Mowern received his *coup de grace* (whilst falling or struggling on the ground to disengage himself from his maimed steed) from the two short, broad-bladed Roman swords.

At length, but not until eight of them had been slain, the others fled in wild disorder from the scene of strife, leaving their king a prisoner in the hands of the foe.

So incensed was Cassivelaunus by this time against him that he ordered his instant execution. In vain Seraptus fell on his knees and begged for mercy. A noose was made in a tethering rope and put over his head, the other end being thrown over the branch of a tree. He was then hauled up off the ground, and in another moment his body was quivering in the air—a corpse.

*　　*　　*　　*　　*　　*

The two Romans received the ardent thanks of King Cassivelaunus for their welcome aid in the brief contest that had just terminated, and then two swift horses being brought forward, and a mounted guide produced, Claudius and Eumolpus took leave of their British friends and set out at full speed for the Roman camp, a good forty-eight hours' journey distant.

King Cassivelaunus, King Cassibelan, Prince Ala, Stella, and the wounded British girl then also mounted their horses, with the determination to return to the still smouldering city.

CHAPTER XXVII.

THE CAMP-FIRE—CLAUDIUS COMBATS WITH A WOLF.

GUIDED by the mounted Briton whom Cassivelaunus had deputed to conduct them with all speed to the Roman camp, Claudius and Eumolpus pressed eagerly forward, the one hope inspiring their hearts that they might be able to reach the army, either in time to warn it of the terrible danger that menaced it, or to perish in the ranks of their comrades.

Men and horses, however, cannot go on for ever without rest and sleep; the first night, therefore, they camped for five hours in a woody dell, hoping to reach the end of their journey by the next evening, but when it came, their guide averred that they were yet far distant from Cæsar's camp, and their horses being regularly knocked up again, they had to encamp in the dark forest.

The guide and Eumolpus the centurion were both soon asleep, but Claudius, who was feverish and restless, lay awake for long hours, and at last felt convinced that he heard the murmur of the sea at no great distance.

If it were so, he reflected that they might be much nearer to Cæsar's camp than the guide imagined, and as the moon shone brightly he determined to walk a little way through the forest, and, if possible, ascertain whether his surmises were correct.

He sprang to his feet, therefore, and wandered on in half-pleased, half-mournful contemplation of the glorious hues of the clouds as ever and anon they burst upon his view in the silvery radiance of the moonlight through the interstices of the wood.

Claudius walked on for more than a mile, but the low moaning roar sounded no nearer, and as by this time he had reluctantly come to the conclusion that it was the wind soughing amidst the highest branches of the forest trees, and not the sea which he had heard, and as the moonlight had gradually died away behind dark clouds, and dark shadows had come creeping over the wood till its thick foliage became black and melancholy, he thought he would retrace his steps.

In the rapidly-increasing gloom he mistook, however, the ambiguous path he had first followed, and the further he pursued the one he had entered upon still more he strayed remotely away into the forest.

While thus perplexed in the mazes of the labyrinth a rustling arose from the thick undergrowth bout him.

He started, drew his sword, and paused for a moment to listen.

The sound ceased, and he stepped a few paces forward again.

Again the sound was audible, and again he stood n the defensive, but once more it ceased, and so nce more he pursued his way, as he thought, towards the camp fire.

But he paused once again for a moment, and hen he could distinctly hear that whatever living hing it was which stirred, whether savage beast r man, it followed his steps, stopped when he topped, and stirred when he stirred, and that so uardedly, that when the sound of his footsteps ied the rustle of its pursuit was also silent.

He stood, therefore, with more caution, and bent his ear towards the ground to listen, and hen only he could hear, though faintly, that his pursuer was gliding on its belly over the clinging moss and through the stunted fern, which carpeted and clothed the ground beneath the underwood.

"It is a wolf!" he exclaimed, and for a moment a cold shiver seemed to run through his veins.

He felt that he was too weary, too weak with strong excitement and great fatigue, to endure the deadly and terrible fray which must ensue if they met.

Besides, a whole pack might be near at hand.

He had not long to dream of fear, however, for the foe approached nearer and nearer still, and the next minute a low, savage growl told him who was the enemy he had to contend with.

Then all his courage returned, and his sinews knit as he clutched his good sword.

A moment more and a crash as if the mighty arm of an oak had been struck to the earth startled the awful silence and made wood and earth vibrate to the sound.

It was plain that the wolf had made a leap for the spot on which he stood, and had alighted short of the mark.

Another low rustle among the underwood, and by the gloomy light of the stars he perceived, and started as he beheld, the eyes of the savage creature glaring their horrid lustre on him.

It was in vain to think of retreat. Courage might do much, but craven cowardice nothing.

With a resolute heart, therefore, he advanced upon his foe.

It was indeed a wolf.

And now came the struggle. With a loud howl, that made the wood re-echo as with the cry of a thousand wolves, the fierce beast advanced upon Claudius, and Claudius upon him.

They were within two paces of each other, reckless man and furious brute.

The wolf gazed at the Standard-Bearer for a moment and then crouched as if to lie down, but his object was to make all the more powerful his leap when he sprang upon his human foe.

In an instant he bounded forward, but the Roman's sword penetrated his shaggy chest.

From the force of the concussion with which

they met Claudius fell to the ground.

With horrid jaws distended, again the wolf sprang upon him, this time wounding him sorely.

He was immediately pinned to the ground, and gave himself up for lost, for the wolf, with its great fangs, had tight hold of his left shoulder, nearly making its teeth meet in his flesh.

Despair made the Roman desperate, but not craven.

Might to might he grappled with the huge beast, and as he was about to give the death bite at his throat, the Roman seized with both hands his tusked jaws, and held him with all his strength.

The wolf's brutal powers meanwhile were not inactive, for Claudius felt the blood trickling down from his torn arms as he lay undermost on the ground, almost stifled with the wolf's weight.

Hope did not, however, entirely forsake him. He struggled till, with a convulsive spring, he flung the wolf from off him, and leapt behind the trunk of a tree which now seemed to stand between him and death.

They were thus parted, and if he could only now deliver one deadly thrust at the wolf's heart Claudius felt that he might yet escape. Thrice he lunged in vain, for thrice the wolf recoiled with a howl from the flashing steel. He returned to the attack, however, each time with more than his former ferociousness. The last desperate effort was made. Claudius stabbed him in the throat, and he fell; he repeated the blow, and exultingly heard the blood gush with a whistling noise from the deep and double-mouthed wound.

The struggle was not over yet, however, for once more the wolf's fangs fastened on the Roman; but it was his last effort, exhausted by the force which was to revenge his overthrow, he fell dead at his conqueror's feet, whose powers, which had been strained beyond the natural strength of man, gave way, and he dropped exhausted across the lifeless carcase of his grim foe.

The dew, however, falling on his face and arms, at last restored Claudius to consciousness. The moon was again shining clear and bright, and here and there her mild, white light glimmered through the topmost boughs of the trees, upon the velvet sward and countless wild flowers beneath.

Claudius remained on the ground until he had recovered his breath, but finding himself presently stronger, he rose to his feet, and determined before the moon again became obscured to endeavour to retrace his steps to the camp-fire and his companions who lay beside it.

With enfeebled steps he resumed the tangled path, and conquering pain with resolution, walked boldly forward in the direction in which he thought the camp-fire lay.

But suddenly he paused, uttering a cry of joy, for through an opening in the wood he beheld the sea, bounded by its yellow belt of sand, and on those sands gleamed the white tents of the Roman army.

Cæsar's camp was scarcely three miles distant, and overjoyed at the discovery he once more turned round, now feeling all his strength and courage returned, to discover the watchfire, and waken and tell Eumolpus.

But long before he reached it, he heard the voice of Eumolpus himself, bellowing aloud his name, and presently encountered him in the midst of a forest glade hurrying to seek him.

The centurion had woke up suddenly from his sleep, and, missing his companion, had at once set out in search of him. The meeting was a most happy one.

Eumolpus bound up the wounds inflicted on the arms of his friend by the fangs and talons of the wolf, and while he was doing so Claudius informed him how near they were to the Roman camp.

The two Romans then determined that they would lose no time, but hurry thitherward at once, before morning broke and daylight rendered their journey more perilous.

They returned to the camp fire, therefore, mounted their horses, and started off immediately, not even troubling to awake their British guide.

CHAPTER XXVIII.

A TERRIBLE BATTLE—A DEAR-BOUGHT VICTORY.

GREY morning dawned in the east, the clouds blushed at the coming of the king of light, and the landscape gleamed afar with the smiles of day.

Not a ripple blurs the surface of the sea, spread out and gleaming like a shield of polished steel.

All is peaceful and beautiful and suggestive of enjoyment or repose, yet, lying close amongst the foxglove and the fern in the dark forest that fringes the shore, long lines of naked or skin-clad Britons are waiting but the signal for assault, and yonder, where the earthwork rises dark and level against the sky, paces to and fro a high-crested sentinel, watching over the safety of the eagles, with the calm and ceaseless vigilance of that discipline which had made the legionaries of Imperial Rome the masters of the world.

Once the trumpets peal—the only sound to be heard in that array of tents, drawn up with such order and precision behind the works, except the footfall of the Roman guard, firm and regular, as it relieves the previous watch.

In a short space that duty will be performed, and then, if ever, must the attack be made with any probability of success.

At length the word is passed from rank to rank in the British host.

Like the crest of a sea wave breaking into foam rises that wavering line of white, naked bodies, rolling its length out like the coils of an immense python, as man after man springs erect at the touch of his comrade, and then a roar of voices, a rush of feet, and the wave sweeps down th rocky slopes, and dashes up to break against the steady, solid resistance of the embankment.

But discipline was not to be caught thus napping.

Ere the echo of their trumpets had died away among the chalk cliffs the legionaries stood to their arms throughout the camp.

Already the rampart gleams and bristles with shield and helmet, javelin, sword, and spear.

Already the eagle is awake and defiant, unruffled indeed, in plumage, but with beak and talons bared and whetted for defence.

The tall centurions marshal their men in line even and regular, as though about to defile by the throne of Cæsar rather than to repel the attack of a wild, barbarian foe.

The tribunes, with their golden crests, take up their appointed posts in the four corners of the camp, while the Emperor himself gives his orders, calm and unmoved, from the centre.

Over the roar of the swarming Britons sounds the clear trumpet note, pealing out in all directions, concise and intelligible as a living voice, and heard by the combatants far and wide, inspiring courage, confidence, and order, even in the midst of confusion.

Brandishing their long swords the naked warriors of Britain rush to the attack.

Already they have filled the ditch and scaled the outwork, but again and again they recoil from the steady front and rigid discipline of the invader, while the short, stabbing sword of the Roman soldier, covered as he is by his ample shield, does fearful execution at close quarters.

But still fresh assailants pour in, and the outward line of circumvallation is carried and overrun.

King Cassivelaunus and King Cassibelan are foremost in the fight; they move as pillars of flashing brightness against the rising sun, scattering light on the yellow shields of the battling host.

The horns of battle bray, the brazen clamour of the regal shields awake the shouts of the mighty ones in fight.

The glancing banners move here and there like the red meteors of the heath.

The warriors of Caer Lud, led by Cassivelaunus, and the Atrebatian braves, headed by Cassibelan, rush downward upon the Roman cohorts, with their glittering arms all raised, like lightning streaming in shattered masses from the dark clouds of midnight—buckler against buckler, and lance against sword, clash like the roar of a thousand thunders!

Who dash on their snorting chargers into the midst of the arrowy tempest—the tumult of the men of strength; where the sharp weapons pour forth showers of blood, and the noise of the battle waxeth louder and louder! Their armour of blocked steel is stained with gore, the plumes of their helms are broken and soiled, but grave and determined are their countenances.

Who are they but Claudius Fulvius, the Standard-Bearer, and Eumolpus, the centurion, who have arrived in time, either to conquer with their comrades, or to die with them?

Their swords glance like gleams of lightning along the dark van of battle.

They rush again and again upon the British host, like thunderbolts dashed against the echoing liffs of some Titanic isle, in an enchanted sea.

The naked barbarians fall in heaps, like showery meteors when the winds rush along the northern skies.

They sink like the waves on the shore, they recoil like the surges of the tide when they go back to the unknown depths of the ocean whence they came.

The Roman army was by this time outnumbered to the extent of ten to one, and the fierce fury of the British onset had, as yet, carried everything before it.

At last the whole camp was in confusion with the exception of the Tenth Legion.

That renowned corps alone stood firm.

The construction of that legion was especially adapted to enhance the self-reliance of well-drilled troops.

It was a small army in itself, containing its proportion of infantry, cavalry, engines of war, and means for conveyance of baggage.

Such a legion, finding itself ever so unexpectedly detached from the main body, was at no loss for those necessaries without which an army melts away like snow in the sunshine, and was capable of independent action in any country, and under any circumstances.

Each man, too, had a perfect confidence in himself and his comrades, and while it was esteemed so high a disgrace to be taken prisoner that many soldiers have been known rather to die by their own hands than to submit to such dishonour, it is not surprising that the Imperial armies have often found means to extricate themselves with credit from positions which would have ensured the destruction of any other troops in the world.

The internal arrangement, too, of every legion, a little perhaps answering to the modern term "division," was calculated to promote individual intelligence and energy in the ranks.

Every soldier not only fought, but fed, slept, marched and toiled under the immediate eye of his *decurion*, or captain of ten, who again was directly responsible for those under his orders to his centurion, or captain of a hundred.

A certain number of these centuries, or companies, varying according to circumstances, constituted a maniple, two of which made up a cohort.

CHAPTER XXIX.

DEATH OF STELLA.

EVERY Roman legion consisted of ten cohorts, under the charge of but six tribunes, who seem to have entered on their onerous office in rotation.

These were again subservient to the general, who, under the different titles of prætor, consul, &c., commanded the whole legion.

The private soldiers were armed with a shield, breastplate, helmet, spear, sword, and dagger, but in addition to his weapons every man carried a set of intrenching tools, and on occasion two or more strong stakes, for the rapid erection of palisades. All were robust labourers, and skilful mechanics as well as invincible combatants.

Against this strong, well-disciplined force it was that the British tide of battle burst and broke, and burst and broke again. When hardest pressed their trumpets would ring out, and in an instant they would form with their shields the figure that was called the tortoise, as a screen against the showers of missiles that would sometimes darken the very air around them.

Cool, confident, and well drilled, they would settle into this impervious order of defence, which consisted in raising their shields obliquely above their heads and linking them together, thus forming an impervious roof of steel, under which they could manœuvre with sufficient freedom. This formation was called the testudo, or tortoise, from its supposed resemblance to the defensive covering with which nature provides that animal.

While, therefore, the rest of the Roman army was fighting in detached cohorts or maniples, surrounded on all sides by thousands of savage warriors thirsting for their blood, looking like islands of burnished steel, which an angry sea of white rolling flesh, crested with floating hair, copper helms, and wildly whirling swords, axes, javelins, and spiked clubs, was striving to bury in its surging tide, the Tenth Legion stood firm as some great rocky headland, rolling back each wave of British valour that surged heavily up against it, with angry moanings and a foam of blood.

The Emperor Cæsar, who was in its centre, noted with pride the conduct of his favourite Legion, though distressed was he beyond measure at the ill success of his troops in other parts of the field. Still no aid could he give them, for on the impenetrability of this one phalanx depended not merely the fate of the day, but the very existence of his army.

As yet the legion, drawn up as it was in front of his beached fleet, had prevented the barbarian foe from approaching near unto his galleys. Did they once succeed in gaining his shipping, and setting fire to the vessels, all chance of escape was impossible, and nought but slavery amongst these islanders, whom they so affected to despise, awaited himself and his army.

From the elevated hillock of sand on which Cæsar stood, utterly regardless of the arrows that flew around him, he could see the golden-haired Cassibelan, at the head of a troop of wild horsemen, thundering down again and again on quivering maniple and cohort, breaking some by the fiery impetuosity of his charge, and recoiling from others, but nothing daunted, to sweep down again a minute later, on their firm foundation, like the very Nemesis of fate.

In another part of the field, too, Cæsar could see the giant King, Cassivelaunus, in a chariot that shone like burnished gold, followed by at least a dozen others, dashing hither and thither, and fighting alternately with spear and sword, while the revolving scythe-blades that were affixed to the hub of each wheel cut down his mailed warriors by scores, and the horrid rattle of the chariots, the snorting of the fiery horses, and the yells of the charioteers, seemed to spread dire consternation in their course.

Then Cæsar at last beheld a sight which gave

him greater joy; it was Claudius Fulvius, the Standard-Bearer, and Eumolpus, the centurion, at the head of at least five hundred Roman horsemen, sweeping to and fro, wherever their comrades were the hardest pressed by the barbarian foe, and with their impetuous and headlong valour restoring hope and confidence where all before was despair.

They and their troop of horse seemed to be in twenty places at once—at one moment thundering down on Cassivelaunus and his war-chariots, causing that redoubtable King to wheel off in another direction; the next galloping to the rescue of some detached cohort or maniple, pressed sore by Cassibelan and his fierce Atrebatian warriors—wherever they charged just turning the tide of battle, though no more.

But the Britons had their horsemen too. There were a thousand Amazons, headed by the Princess Stella, whose long hair floated in the wind or fell in rich clustering tresses over her naked breast; and there was another force nearly equal in number, composed of youths under twenty, which was commanded by the boy-Prince, Ala, of Caer Lud.

A near observer might have noticed that Claudius and his mailed warriors took great trouble to avoid both these bands of barbarian cavalry, and Cæsar himself was not slow to discover this fact. Once or twice he asked one or other of his surrounding officers, "Who was that dashing Amazon, with the snow-white and beautifully-proportioned body, with the helmet of gold and the rich brown hair that floated beneath it; who again and again led thousand half-naked Amazons so gallantly to the charge?"

At last, however, a collision between her followers and the rough warriors of Claudius became inevitable. She had given the command to charge, not knowing who he was who led that stern array. She discovered it too late, nor did Claudius dare to order his men to fly from a herd of wild women.

With a wild yell, and in one fierce rushing disorderly charge, the Amazons were sweeping down upon his little band, and he could not but command his men to abide the onslaught.

With lifted shields and levelled spears, the two bodies of horse rushed to meet each other, Claudius spurring a good couple of lengths in front of his men, hoping that he might encounter Stella in person, and force her to yield herself prisoner to him before she got wounded or slain in the melée.

But it was not to be. On came the Amazons, flourishing their weapons above their heads, each one a thorough master of her horse, and sitting as upright as a centaur on its unsaddled back. On they came, an imposing array of warlike beauty, but with flushed cheeks, and cruel and merciless eyes, that showed that they neither meant to give or to accept quarter.

Already Claudius and Stella had recognised each other, but the latter, putting all human affection aside in her love and duty to her country, merely bestowed upon him a sorrowing glance, and then rode right at him, with her gleaming copper sword, and her round white arm raised to strike.

The Standard-Bearer rushed at her, intending to dash the sword from her hand with a strong blow, then to kill her steed, and as the animal fell, to drag her across his own horse and fight his way out of the melée, and protecting her body from friend and foe alike, until he could deposit her in some safe place.

But alas, his kindly intentions were doomed to be defeated, for at the very moment of their encounter, Claudius's right-hand man, not knowing the relationship in which his young leader and the fair British girl stood towards each other, urged his horse forward, and with his long spear transfixed her through the chest, the cruel steel coming out several inches behind her back.

She was not unhorsed however, for Claudius dashed alongside and sustained her in his arms, and her assailant, having quitted hold of his spear and galloped away sword in hand against other foes, Claudius cleft it in twain with a stroke of his sword, and then essayed to withdraw it from Stella's body.

Her agony must have been intense, but closing her lover's grasp within her own around the spear, she bid him draw it quickly forth so that she might die in his arms.

For a moment he hesitated; but she flung her white arms around his neck, and leant her cheek against his, and then Claudius could tell by the terrible tremor that ran through her form, that the quicker her pain was ended the more merciful would it be. He, therefore, even while pressing her closer to his embrace and venturing for the first time to kiss her warm cheek, gently withdrew the spear from her body.

Directly he had done so the blood welled up in dark red jets, and then began to pour forth as it cleared its channel, in one continuous stream that in a minute drained life away. With a quiver of her dainty limbs, with a smile deepening in her fair face, and with her fond eyes fixed on his, and her half-opened lips breathing every instant fainter and fainter against his cheek, the spirit of that beautiful but ill-fated British Princess passed into eternity, and Claudius lifting her body on to his own horse, galloped away with it, nor stayed until he gained the reserve of the British host, where he rendered it into the care of some wounded warriors of Atrebatium, at the same time of necessity yielding himself up a prisoner.

* * * * *

Meanwhile, Prince Ala at the head of his youthful chivalry, would be content with nothing else but leading them against the adamantine walls of the Tenth Legion. They charged down with a tremendous cheer; but once and again they recoil from the steady front and rigid discipline of the Roman phalanx.

Ala, however, will not be discouraged; a last final effort to break that firm and hitherto invincible array he determines to make. He addresses a few spirit-stirring words to his followers; again they rush on.

Ala lifts his fleet horse to a leap, and it bounds right over the heads of the outermost rank of the

Romans, descending on their upraised shields, like a thunderbolt, and breaking for an instant their hitherto impervious line of steel.

A moment's confusion was sufficient to enable Ala's youthful band of nearly nine hundred followers to rush within the cordon after their leader, who never glanced back to see whether they were behind.

The young warrior rushed exultingly to and fro, and the enemy fell in heaps before him.

Such moments are worth whole years of peaceful life.

He has pierced five ranks of the foe. He is close beneath the eagles, and he leaps wildly at them to bring them off in triumph as trophies of his victory, as a gift to his father, the King of Caer Lud.

But, lo, just as he grasps the shaft of an eagle-guidoned standard in his hand, a grim centurion strikes him to the earth.

Wounded, faint and bleeding, he is made a prisoner; his wild cries to his companions to hasten to his rescue are unheard, for they are already in full retreat, only too glad to get outside the Roman phalanx with the loss of three-fourths of their number; and it closes grimly in their rear, impenetrable as ever.

* * * * *

But why dwell at greater length on the records of that day of days?

The fierce contest lasted from the rising of the sun until the going down of the same. Cohort after cohort, legion after legion, of the Roman army is defeated.

Cassibelan has seized the golden eagle of the Ninth, Cassivelaunus the gorgeous standard of the Eighth Legions; they wave them above their heads, then mount, the one his charger the other his chariot, and raise their shouts of triumph.

The fierce Britons pursue their discomfited foemen like a band of wolves chasing the sheep-flocks in the flowery vales of the Avon or the Severn.

And yet the Roman army is not conquered; though the Britons have defeated maniple after maniple, cohort after cohort, legion after legion, the glorious Tenth, Cæsar's own, still remains as a column of granite, invincible, unbreakable!

They held their ground from daylight until darkness set in, and then the Britons were fain to leave them masters of the field.

But even then the naked warriors of the north spared neither the feeble nor the wounded. The sun sank from the heavens, and with it died the wailings of despair; it set on the silent city of death, and there was no one to weep over the slain, no man to bury the dead.

The eagle and the wolf were gorged with feasting that night, the forest bear ate of the flesh of the strong and mighty, and the horn-beaked raven croaked for joy over the banquet of blood.

The Britons encamped once more on the borders of the grim forests that overlooked the sea. At daybreak on the morrow they intended again to sweep down upon the Roman invader, and on that, the third day of battle, to drive into the sea, or put to the sword every man that survived.

But when morn broke, lo! the Roman camp was deserted, for the Tenth Legion had succeeded in noiselessly launching the galleys during the hours of darkness, and now their silken sails were only barely discernible against the deep blue of the distant horizon.

The Legion had saved its honour, its eagles, its Emperor, and at least three-forths of its warriors.

CHAPTER XXX.

ONCE MORE WITHIN THE ROMAN COLOSSEUM!

A HUNDRED thousand tongues, whispering and murmuring with Italian volubility, sent up a busy hum like that of an enormous beehive into the sunny air.

Such was the enormous crowd of human beings high and low assembled in the vast amphitheatre of the Colosseum that when any motion went through the assembly the noise of their rising up or sitting down could be likened to nothing except, perhaps, the far-off sullen roaring of the illimitable sea or the rushing of a great night wind among the boughs of a forest.

For any one who had never seen a peopled amphitheatre, or beheld a very great multitude of men assembled together within any fabric of human erection, there was in the scene now presented enough to impress his mind with a very strange feeling of astonishment, not to say of veneration.

Not less than a hundred thousand human beings, and such was the stupendous capacity of the building, that it was not in the least over-crowded, were assembled here together.

Such a multitude could nowhere be regarded without inspiring a certain indefinite and indefinable sense of majesty, least of all when congregated together within the wide sweep of such a glorious edifice as this, and surrounded on all sides with every circumstance of ornament and splendour befitting an everlasting monument of Roman victories, the munificence of Roman princes, and the imperial luxury of universal Rome.

Julius Cæsar himself has already taken his seat on his ivory throne, and the sunshine blazing in through a rift in the awning that is stretched high overhead, deepens the broad crimson hem that encircles his imperial robes, and renders less stern the iron profile of his countenance.

A peal of trumpets, a clash of cymbals, a burst of wild martial music rising above the hum and murmur of the seething crowd, and a door on the right hand of the arena was laid open and a single trumpet sounded mournfully, while the gladiators marched in with slow steps, each man naked except being girt with a cloth about his loins, bearing on his left arm a small buckler, and having a short straight sword suspended by a cord around his neck.

They marched slowly and steadily, so that the whole assembly had full leisure wherein to contemplate the forms of the men, while those who were or imagined themselves to be skilled in the business of the arena were fixing in their own minds on such as they thought would be victorious, and laying wagers concerning their chances of success with as much unconcern as if they had been contemplating so many irrational animals, or rather indeed so many senseless pieces of ingenious mechanism.

The wide diversity of complexion and feature exhibited among these devoted athletes afforded at once a majestic idea of the extent of the Roman empire, and a terrible one of the purposes to which that wide sway had been too often made subservient.

The beautiful Greek, with countenance of noble serenity, and limbs after which the sculptors of his country might have modelled their god-like statues, walked side by side with the yellow-bearded savage whose gigantic muscles had been nerved in the freezing waves of the Elbe or the Danube, or whose thick strong hair was congealed and shagged on his brow with the breath of Scythian or Scandinavian winters.

Many fierce Moors and Arabs and curly-locked Ethiopians were there, with the beams of the southern sun burnt in every various shade of swarthiness upon their skins. Nor did Britain's sea-girt isle want her representatives in the deadly procession; for among the armed multitude were two or three gaunt barbarians whose breast and shoulders bore uncouth devices tattooed with blue woad, so vivid in their tints that probably many months had not elapsed since they were wandering in wild freedom along the native ridges of some oak forest, or fighting Rome's legions on the Kentish beach.

As they marched around the arena they were saluted by the whole multitude with noisy acclamations in token of the approbation wherewith their feats at some former festival stamped them with renown and made them worthy of being remembered.

But on the appearance of others, groans and hisses were heard from all parts of the amphitheatre, mixed with contending cheers from others of the spectators; but by far the greater part were suffered to pass on in silence, this being in all likelihood the first—alas! who could not tell, whether it might or might not also be the last—day of their sharing in such a fearful exhibition.

After their parading around the lists, they halt abruptly before Cæsar's throne, and brandishing their gleaming weapons above their heads shout as with one voice—

"*Ave Cæsar Imperator! Morituri te salutant!*"

Then they wheel out once more into the centre of the arena, the fencing-masters pair them, and in succession they begin to give proof of their fatal skill.

At first Scythian is matched against Scythian, Greek against Greek, Ethiopian against Ethiopian, Spaniard against Spaniard, and the sand is presently dyed red beneath their feet, with the blood streaming from the wounds inflicted by kindred hands.

But these combats, although abundantly bloody and terrible, are regarded only as preludes to the serious business of the day, which was to consist of duels between Europeans on the one side and Asiatics and Africans on the other, wherein the well-nigh intransgressible law of the amphitheatre was laid down that at least one out of every pair of combatants should die on the sands of the arena, before the eyes of the multitude, whether they signified that the victim was to be spared or no.

Instead of shrinking from the more desperate brutalities of these latter conflicts, the almost certainty of their fatal termination seemed only to make the assembly gaze on them with a more intense curiosity and a more inhuman measure of delight.

At last sickened with the protracted terrors of a conflict that seemed as if it were never to have an end, although both the combatants were already covered all over with hideous gashes, some women did faint or scream, whilst others bowed down their heads or clasped their hands upon their eyes to save them from the torture of gazing further thereon.

At that instant all were silent in the contemplation of the barbarous strife, insomuch that a groan, the first that had escaped from either of the combatants, although low and reluctant and half suppressed, sounded quite distinctly amid the deep hush of the assembly, and being constrained thereby to turn their eyes once more downwards, they beheld that at length one of the two had received the sword of his adversary quite through his body, and had sunk before him on the sand.

A beautiful young man was he who had received this hurt, with fair hair clustering in glossy ringlets upon his neck and brows, but the sickness of his wound was already visible on his drooping eyelids, and his lips were pale, as if the blush had rushed from them to the untimely outlet.

Nevertheless, the Moorish gladiator who had fought with him had drawn forth again his weapon, and stood there awaiting in silence the decision of the multitude, whether at once to slay the defenceless youth, or to assist in removing him from the arena, if perchance the blood might be stopped from flowing, and some hope of recovery even yet extended to him.

Thereupon there arose on the instant a loud voice of contention, and the wounded man regarded the multitude with a proud and withal a contemptuous glance, being aware that without question he had executed all things so as to deserve their compassion, but aware, moreover, that even had that been freely vouchsafed to him, it was too late for any hope of recovery, for he was fast bleeding to death.

But the cruelty of their faces, it may be, and the loudness of their cries, were a sorrow to him, and filled his dying breast with loathing and disgust.

Whether or not the haughtiness of his countenance had been observed by them with displeasure is uncertain, but so it was that those who had cried out at first for mercy became speedily silent, and the Emperor, looking around, and seeing all the thumbs turned downwards (the signal of death) was constrained to give the sign, and forthwith the young gladiator, receiving again the sword blade of the Moor into his gashed bosom, breathed forth his life, and lay stretched out upon the yellow sands of the arena.

With that a joyous clamour was uplifted by many of those that 'oked upon it, and the victorious Moor, being crowned with an ivy garland, was carried in procession around the arena by certain young men who leaped down for the purpose from the midst of the plebeian circle of benches which surrounded one half of the amphitheatre.

In the meantime those that had the care of such things dragged away with a filthy hook the corpse of him that had been slain, and then raking up the sand over the blood that had fallen from him prepared the place with indifferent countenances for the next cruel tragedy, while all around the spectators were seen rising from their places and saluting each other, and there was a buzz of talking as universal as the silence had been during the combat, some speaking of it and paying and receiving money lost and won upon its issue, some already laughing merrily, and discoursing concerning other matters, even as if nothing uncommon had been witnessed, while others again appeared to be entirely occupied with the martial music, which ever struck up majestically at such pauses in the course of the cruel exhibition, some beating time upon the benches before them, others lightly joining their voices in union with the proud notes of the trumpets and the silver clarions.

* * * * * ^

But a different species of combat is now to ensue; a portable wooden cage is borne into the arena, and its iron-barred front being turned towards Cæsar's throne and the patrician benches, they can perceive a long low, dark object lying coiled up inside, and presently they can make out the fawning, cruel head, the glaring eyes, and the striped sinewy form of a large tiger.

The attendants who bore in the cage lift up the grating and rush away from the spot with the rapidity of men in peril of their lives, leaping the six-foot-high barrier into the lower benches.

Then there enters the arena a noble-looking youth, naked save for a cincture around his loins, with a form worthy of a Grecian statue, and a skin as soft, white, and fair as that of a girl.

He is armed with a sword, shield, and helmet, and advances towards the tiger with a bold and menacing style; his buckler well advanced, and his sword-point threatening his grim foe.

Stay, we have seen that handsome stripling's face before. It is Prince Ala of Caer Lud, to whom the Emperor Cæsar has promised deliverance from slavery, and a safe return to his father's kingdom, if, naked and armed as he is, he can succeed in conquering the Libyan tiger.

Vain mockery of pardon! Not one man out of a hundred, meeting a strong tiger with such weapons as his, could hope to overcome the powerful brute, much less a mere boy.

The young Briton's rounded limbs gleam with the oil wherewith they have been anointed, as he stands in the centre of the arena, awaiting the tiger's charge; but in vain he waits for his fourfooted foe to begin the attack. Although the monster is sufficiently hungry, having been kept for three days without food, he skulks under the barrier, for 'tis not his nature to carry on an open warfare.

Ala disdains to wait for long; his patience is short—short almost as that of the audience, who are breathlessly waiting to see his white polished limbs torn to pieces.

He advances upon the tiger with quick steps and undaunted mien.

There is a flash like real fire from the tiger's eyes, hitherto only sullen and watchful; his waving tail describes a semicircle in the sand, and he coils himself more and more closely together, with a deep low growl, for even now he is not disposed to fight save at an advantage.

A hundred thousand pairs of eyes, straining eagerly on the combatants, could scarce detect the exact moment at which that fearful spring was made.

All they can now discern is the British Prince on his back, and with his upraised shield keeping the tiger from his throat.

His legs, from knees to ankles, are already lacerated by the brute's hinder claws, and there is an expression of acute agony on his youthful countenance as he feels that death is certain.

But a wild shout, like unto nothing but an Indian war-cry, rings through the amphitheatre, and a warrior, all glittering in brass, steel, and scarlet, leaps like a blazing meteor adown tier after tier of seats, and finally springs over the barrier into the whirling dust and sand of the arena.

"A legionary! a legionary!" shout the populace, while some hiss and some applaud his daring.

He heeds them not, but rushes straightway upon the tiger.

A deep gash upon its tawny shoulder causes the fierce beast to turn upon its new adversary.

Again it essays its deadly spring, but this time it is to rush upon a firmly-held sword that pierces its broad breast to the very heart, and the rescuer, withdrawing the blood-red blade, plants his foot proudly on the tiger's corpse.

Prince Ala then springs from the sand, and dashes down sword and buckler, as he recognises in his deliverer from a horrid death Claudius Fulvius, the Standard-Bearer.

But angry murmurs by this time arise on all sides, for Claudius has dared to interfere with the course of the sports, and a lictor approaches to conduct him and the Briton before Cæsar's throne.

Arrived there, however, the Emperor was so glad to see his favourite Standard-Bearer, whom he thought had been slain in that last fearful day of carnage on the sands of Britain, that he received him more like a brother than an humble legionary, and promised him what boon he might ask.

"Give, then, this brave boy his freedom, my Emperor, and ensure his safe return to his father's court in Britain. I have been a prisoner in that fair island for twelve long months, but have been treated with kindness, and at last set at liberty without ransom. Act equally nobly by this boy, I pray thee."

And Cæsar granted the request of Claudius Fulvius, and, furthermore, in time made him a

Tribune—an office which he filled with credit to the day of his death, many years after.

Claudius had only arrived in Rome and entered the amphitheatre in time to save Ala's life.

Retiring from Cæsar's throne, he was speedily clasped in the arms of a father, whom, it will be remembered, his bravery had caused the Emperor to recall from banishment and restore to his favour.

Eumolpus greeted him, too, as one returned from the dead, and he found dozens of the friends of his youth waiting to carry him on their shoulders in triumph to his father's palace by the Tiber.

THE END.